Anthony Gilbert and The Murder Room

》》 This title is part of The Murder Room, our series dedicated to making available out-of-print or hard-to-find titles by classic crime writers.

Crime fiction has always held up a mirror to society. The Victorians were fascinated by sensational murder and the emerging science of detection; now we are obsessed with the forensic detail of violent death. And no other genre has so captivated and enthralled readers.

Vast troves of classic crime writing have for a long time been unavailable to all but the most dedicated frequenters of second-hand bookshops. The advent of digital publishing means that we are now able to bring you the backlists of a huge range of titles by classic and contemporary crime writers, some of which have been out of print for decades.

From the genteel amateur private eyes of the Golden Age and the femmes fatales of pulp fiction, to the morally ambiguous hard-boiled detectives of mid twentieth-century America and their descendants who walk our twenty-first century streets, The Murder Room has it all. **》》**

The Murder Room
Where Criminal Minds Meet

themurderroom.com

T0345412

Anthony Gilbert (1899–1973)

Anthony Gilbert was the pen name of Lucy Beatrice Malleson. Born in London, she spent all her life there, and her affection for the city is clear from the strong sense of character and place in evidence in her work. She published 69 crime novels, 51 of which featured her best known character, Arthur Crook, a vulgar London lawyer totally (and deliberately) unlike the aristocratic detectives, such as Lord Peter Wimsey, who dominated the mystery field at the time. She also wrote more than 25 radio plays, which were broadcast in Great Britain and overseas. Her thriller *The Woman in Red* (1941) was broadcast in the United States by CBS and made into a film in 1945 under the title *My Name is Julia Ross*. She was an early member of the British Detection Club, which, along with Dorothy L. Sayers, she prevented from disintegrating during World War II. Malleson published her autobiography, *Three-a-Penny*, in 1940, and wrote numerous short stories, which were published in several anthologies and in such periodicals as *Ellery Queen's Mystery Magazine* and *The Saint*. The short story 'You Can't Hang Twice' received a Queens award in 1946. She never married, and evidence of her feminism is elegantly expressed in much of her work.

By Anthony Gilbert

Scott Egerton series

Tragedy at Freyne (1927)

The Murder of Mrs
  Davenport (1928)

Death at Four Corners (1929)

The Mystery of the Open
  Window (1929)

The Night of the Fog (1930)

The Body on the Beam (1932)

The Long Shadow (1932)

The Musical Comedy
  Crime (1933)

An Old Lady Dies (1934)

The Man Who Was Too
  Clever (1935)

**Mr Crook Murder
  Mystery series**

Murder by Experts (1936)

The Man Who Wasn't
  There (1937)

Murder Has No Tongue (1937)

Treason in My Breast (1938)

The Bell of Death (1939)

Dear Dead Woman (1940)
  aka *Death Takes a Redhead*

The Vanishing Corpse (1941)
  aka *She Vanished in the Dawn*

The Woman in Red (1941)
  aka *The Mystery of the
  Woman in Red*

Death in the Blackout (1942)
  aka *The Case of the Tea-
  Cosy's Aunt*

Something Nasty in the
  Woodshed (1942)
  aka *Mystery in the Woodshed*

The Mouse Who Wouldn't
  Play Ball (1943)
  aka *30 Days to Live*

He Came by Night (1944)
  aka *Death at the Door*

The Scarlet Button (1944)
  aka *Murder Is Cheap*

A Spy for Mr Crook (1944)

The Black Stage (1945)
  aka *Murder Cheats the Bride*

Don't Open the Door (1945)
  aka *Death Lifts the Latch*

Lift Up the Lid (1945)
  aka *The Innocent Bottle*

The Spinster's Secret (1946)
  aka *By Hook or by Crook*

Death in the Wrong Room
  (1947)

Die in the Dark (1947)
  aka *The Missing Widow*

Death Knocks Three Times
  (1949)

Murder Comes Home (1950)

A Nice Cup of Tea (1950)
  aka *The Wrong Body*

Lady-Killer (1951)

Miss Pinnegar Disappears (1952)
 aka *A Case for Mr Crook*

Footsteps Behind Me (1953)
 aka *Black Death*

Snake in the Grass (1954)
 aka *Death Won't Wait*

Is She Dead Too? (1955)
 aka *A Question of Murder*

And Death Came Too (1956)

Riddle of a Lady (1956)

Give Death a Name (1957)

Death Against the Clock (1958)

Death Takes a Wife (1959)
 aka *Death Casts a Long Shadow*

Third Crime Lucky (1959)
 aka *Prelude to Murder*

Out for the Kill (1960)

She Shall Die (1961)
 aka *After the Verdict*

Uncertain Death (1961)

No Dust in the Attic (1962)

Ring for a Noose (1963)

The Fingerprint (1964)

The Voice (1964)
 aka *Knock, Knock! Who's There?*

Passenger to Nowhere (1965)

The Looking Glass Murder (1966)

The Visitor (1967)

Night Encounter (1968)
 aka *Murder Anonymous*

Missing from Her Home (1969)

Death Wears a Mask (1970)
 aka *Mr Crook Lifts the Mask*

Murder is a Waiting Game (1972)

Tenant for the Tomb (1971)

A Nice Little Killing (1974)

Standalone Novels

The Case Against Andrew Fane (1931)

Death in Fancy Dress (1933)

The Man in the Button Boots (1934)

Courtier to Death (1936)
 aka *The Dover Train Mystery*

The Clock in the Hatbox (1939)

And Death Came Too

Anthony Gilbert

This edition published by
The Orion Publishing Group Ltd
Orion House
5 Upper St Martin's Lane
London WC2H 9EA

An Hachette UK company
A CIP catalogue record for this book is available from the British Library

ISBN 978 1 4719 1004 3

www.orionbooks.co.uk

Affectionately to
Mr and Mrs Harry Maule

1

On an afternoon in September 1948 Mr Thomas ('London')
Fogg, K.C., sat in the saloon bar of the Two Chairmen talking
to his friend, Mr Arthur (My-clients-are-always-innocent) Crook.
The two men made a piquant contrast, Fogg being small, sober,
wearing excellent if baggy conventional clothes, with a ridicu-
lously high intellectual forehead, aggressive nose and square
mouth—(Catch a couple of rats in that, Crook used to say) and
small dark eyes set very far back under shaggy brows, while his
companion was conspicuous in any society by reason of his
flaming red hair, thick brows over eyes as round and brown as
brandy-balls and the regrettably loud shade of chocolate brown
suiting he invariably affected. Fogg was drinking marsala, while
Crook stuck to beer. As might have been expected, Fogg was
doing the talking.

'A point that has always troubled me, Crook,' he said in
emphatic tones, 'is how far we have discharged our duty to our
clients when we have merely succeeded in getting them a verdict
that does not at the same time offer tangible proof of innocence.
Not Guilty so often implies Not Proven, with most unsatisfactory
consequences for the person concerned.'

'It's all according,' demurred Crook, picking up his glass and
emptying the contents down his throat as though, thought his
companion, fascinated, he were watering a flower-bed. 'We
get them freedom and the future, and they ain't to be sneezed
at.'

'Freedom and the future,' repeated the K.C. reflectively. 'But
freedom for what? and a future worth how much? It can't have
escaped your attention, my dear fellow, that the aftermath of a
murder trial that has resulted in an acquittal, mainly for lack of
proof of guilt, only too often implies virtual ostracism for the
discharged prisoner.' He named two or three well-known cases

of recent years, in each of which the accused man had been given the benefit of the doubt. In each case he had found himself unable to follow his previous calling, owing to local prejudice or frank disbelief in his innocence.

'They don't usually last long,' Mr Fogg continued. 'No incentive to go on living, perhaps.'

'Guilty conscience perhaps,' suggested Crook callously. 'If you ask me, it's downright careless to get yourself arrested for murder in the first place. No one thinks less of the police than I do, but even I have to admit they don't go out picking people up without some good reason. You've never been arrested for a murder, Fogg, nor have I. Trouble is people will complicate their lives by falling in love in the wrong quarter. . . .' He paused abruptly, at the sight of Mr Fogg's face. 'You really have got something on your mind, haven't you?' he urged.

'I am gravely troubled,' agreed Mr Fogg in his deliberate old-fashioned manner. 'It is serious enough when the victim—you will agree, I take it, that that is a fair description—is a middle-aged person, well established in life, but when it is a young girl with no background and, so far as I can see, absolutely no chance of proving her innocence—yes, my heart is very heavy. I have a sense, Crook, that I've failed that girl, yet for the life of me I can't see what more I could have done.'

'I heard you'd taken a case up north,' said Crook—very little escaped him. 'Was that the job?'

'That as you say, was the job. You yourself hold such an enviable record (Pedantic old buster, thought Crook affectionately, mutely inviting the barman to fill up both their glasses) that I should welcome your advice.'

'Puttin' the cart before the horse, ain't you?' said Crook, looking as surprised as he ever allowed himself to be. 'The Counsel's the big noise in these court cases, or so I've always been led to believe.'

'That, my dear fellow, is ridiculous, and, if I may say so, quite untrue. It it well known that all the spade-work and a large proportion of the success of a criminal case is the credit of the solicitor. You have the reputation of never losing a client—to the gallows, I mean. I have even heard you say that where the requisite evidence is not forthcoming you are prepared to manufacture it. I'm wondering whether you could have produced sufficient evidence in the case of Rex v. Garside to have won my client a definite verdict of Not Guilty.'

'Any evidence to start with?' enquired Crook, accepting the challenge as gay as a lark. 'I can make bricks with as little straw as any man, but even I need a little.'

'If you will cast your mind back to the Wallace case in the early 'thirties you may recall that the prosecution adduced a number of facts all of which seemed virtually to prove that the prisoner must be guilty of the murder of his wife. And then Counsel for the Defence, using precisely the same facts, appeared to show that they quite as probably proved his innocence. In the case of Miss Garside, the Crown could show that she had means, motive and opportunity in ample measure. Her alleged victim was her own father, and parricide, or even attempted parricide, is not well looked on in this country.'

'She should have been born in ancient Greece,' retorted Crook, blatantly, with a vague memory of the classics. 'Or do I mean Rome? Never mind that,' he added in a hurried voice. 'Why did she want to get rid of the old buster?'

'Andrew Garside must be as callous and self-indulgent an old monster as any man I've had the misfortune to meet,' returned Fogg, in his usual calm tones. 'One could only applaud the enterprise of any young girl who tried to get away from him. But poison is not the method one would advise. It's always a disadvantage when poison is the vehicle employed,' he continued, 'because it argues premeditation. I suppose a large percentage of the human race would be capable of murder on impulse, if the provocation were sufficiently great and the opportunity sufficiently glaring. But premeditated murder arouses sympathy in no one.'

'Specially when it's your old man,' Crook concurred. 'Ha, here comes the second round. Drink up, Fogg, and let's get down to brass tacks. You've done your song and dance, and very pretty they were. Now ring up the curtain.'

Thus adjured, Mr Fogg told his story.

'Miss Garside—Ruth—is the only child of her father's disastrous second marriage. She is now twenty, whereas he was past fifty when she was born. I understand he took no interest in her at the time and has shown no interest in her since, at all events not until she became an heiress in a small way.'

'Papa not having much to bless himself with?' suggested Crook.

'I should doubt if Andrew Garside has ever done a stroke of work since he came down from Cambridge fifty years ago. His own means were very small, but he solved the problem of survival by marrying a lady fifteen years older than himself. I should add that he has one quality that's always good for a handsome return. That is charm. Even now, at 73, though admittedly he looks considerably less, he could coax a hippopotamus out of its pond during a heat-wave. He is also extremely good-looking. Apart from that he has nothing whatsoever to commend him. However, ladies being what they are, he had no difficulty in marrying money and obtaining the use of it during the ten years that his marriage lasted. I am also quite convinced that the first Mrs Garside considered she had made an excellent bargain. There were no children of the marriage, and when the lady died she left every penny to her husband. He didn't marry again, not for a considerable time, that is, but settled down to a pleasant, even a luxurious bachelor existence. He maintained a comfortable establishment, travelled, rode, hunted, played an excellent game of bridge and kept a fine cellar—it was possible to do all these things on an income of £2,000 before the First World War. Like the grasshopper, he doesn't appear to have considered the future much and was caught by the slump in the 'thirties. As I've said, he was quite incapable of earning a living, so he took the only step open to him . . .'

'And married money for the second time?' chipped in the irrepressible Crook.

'Precisely. This time the disparity in age was even greater but on what the world considers the right side. Mary Roult was the only child of a well-to-do merchant who had left her with a very tidy fortune but, as one used to say, no social background. She was 23 and was immensely flattered, I should imagine, by the attentions of this handsome unscrupulous middle-aged rogue, and married him out of hand. That marriage was a failure almost from the start. You realise I only have all this information at second-hand, but Dick Devenish, who provided the brief, had gone into the facts with some thoroughness, and I'm indebted to him for what I know. It was one of these cases where the background is of very great importance. Ruth was born at the end of the first year; before the marriage was three years old Mrs Garside had left her husband, saying that she'd freeze to death if she stayed with him any longer.'

'So off she went where the welcome would be warmer?' hazarded Crook.

Fogg looked faintly displeased at this colloquial interpretation of his remarks. 'My dear fellow, can you not say what you mean?' he demanded with some asperity. 'She fled with a lover, leaving her child to that heartless old reprobate, a course for which it's hard not to blame her, though, never having had the misfortune to live with Garside at close quarters it's difficult to estimate the precise provocation. One gathers that Garside's chief preoccupation was the disposal of his wife's fortune. She had lawyers who had insisted on tying up her money, possibly anticipating just such a development; the long and the short of it is, he couldn't touch a penny. I believe he would have disowned the girl if he could, but that was out of the question. He revenged himself on his wife by refusing to give her a divorce, and cast about for some way of preserving his own comfort. Eventually he persuaded an unmarried sister, living very contentedly in the South of England, to sell up her home and come north— for the sake of the child, he said. Miss Garside had her own small fortune, and if he wasn't so well-endowed as before he was still able to keep a car and a good cellar, entertain and dress well. It's notable that he didn't send the girl to school, saying that his sister had been a schoolmistress before she inherited her unexpected legacy and was perfectly capable of educating the little girl. That matter, of course, arose later. Ruth was only two years old when Miss Garside came to the house. For thirteen years she was an exemplary stepmother—if the word can be employed—to her brother's child. Ruth's life may have been an unconventional one and, by normal standards, lonely, but she seems to have been quite happy. Miss Garside exerted herself to find a few companions of Ruth's own age and if she hadn't been stricken with some mortal disease about five years ago this case would never have come into court. This happened,

of course, in the middle of the war. The war disrupted everybody's life, even Andrew had to forgo some of his comforts. It
was an odd household, in some ways as odd as that of the
Brontës. The old man lived quite apart from the rest, and his
daughter saw remarkably little of him. Miss Garside wanted to go
into a hospital when she realised the seriousness of her condition, but Andrew put his foot down. Hospitals cost money, a
deal more money than it would cost to nurse her at home.
Events were with him. Beds in hospital were hard to get, civilian
nurses grossly overworked. Ruth was fifteen, too young for
national service, but not, in her father's eyes, too young to nurse
a woman dying of a horrible disease. This state of affairs lasted
for about six months, and then Miss Garside died, having been
under morphia during the last weeks of her life.'

'I take it that's important,' said Crook.

'It's the crux of the situation. When the will came to be read
Garside was incredulous with rage to hear that his sister had left
all her money to her niece. He tried to get it upset, on the ground
of mental derangement, but it was more than two years old. His
only satisfaction was that, so long as his daughter was a minor,
the income was at his disposal. The capital he couldn't touch.
When Ruth was 21 it was hers to make ducks and drakes of, if she
liked, and there was a provision that if she married before attain-
ing her majority, the money should be administered by her legal
representative, that is, this fellow, Devenish, I mentioned just
now.'

'So it was in Dad's interest to keep her away from any
eligibles,' contributed Crook.

'Precisely. The income wasn't large and the cost of living was
on the increase. There was also income-tax, so Mr Garside had
to pull in his horns. He gave up the house in which they'd been
living and rented a small remote cottage, where the girl was
completely cut off. He contrived to get a petrol ration for his car
and spent much of his time in the nearest town. It was impossible to get any help, the girl was over 15 so no School Officer
could intervene, there was never any question of physical ill-
treatment and during the war everyone was working full-stretch.
In a word, she could have died and been buried, and no one
would have noticed, except Andrew Garside. It's an extraordinary

situation to arise at the present time,' he added, contemplatively. 'But it can't be without precedent. If there had been school friends or anyone to take a particular interest in her, matters would have been different, but even evacuees didn't penetrate to that solitary place. I've seen the cottage, it's set on the lip of a valley, one of those abysses that are attributed to some convulsion of the earth in the Ice Age when the face of the land was split asunder and a great valley created . . . There are a few farms round there and a small village some distance below, but since there was no bus service during the war she was almost completely isolated. It's not strange that a girl growing up in such conditions, a girl moreover capable of very strong feelings, should become . . .' he hesitated, 'eccentric is rather too strong a word, but she was cast back upon herself at every turn, and she is a girl capable of great passion. I don't pretend to any especial psychological insight, but I do think it is a tragedy of the first water that she should have had no natural outlet during those formative years.'

He drained his second glass of marsala, and went on more quickly. 'We come to 1946, when she was 18, and struck out for herself for the first time. It was one of the anomalies of the situation that though the money was legally hers she saw practically nothing of it. She had no new clothes, no pleasures, no comforts, and so suddenly she sold a brooch her aunt had left her, bought a bicycle and found herself employment with a local doctor called Stocks. Her father, I gather, was altogether antagonistic to the scheme, but she was 18 and he couldn't prevent her. From Ruth's point of view it was an excellent move. The Stocks were kindly people with a family of young children; she was soon at home in the household, helping Mrs Stocks when she wasn't dispensing for the doctor—her way of life had made her remarkably old for her years, and in those remote parts life is conducted with rather less red tape than we're accustomed to in towns—and she was frequently invited to small jollifications.'

Crook put out a big hand over his mouth to hide a grin at that old-fashioned word. He couldn't imagine that the jollifications in question were anything but pretty sober affairs.

'Andrew Garside did his level best to put a stop to these

social occasions,' continued Mr Fogg, unmoved. 'He discovered a damaged heart, which must have come as a surprise to his daughter who had had no reason to suppose he possessed such an organ; he was constantly urging her early return or demanding that she should give up her work on his account. But the girl, having tasted a little freedom, took the bit between her teeth. If her father was really a sick man, she suggested, let them abandon the cottage and live nearer civilisation. Andrew pointed out that their means were very restricted and expenses still increasing. Ruth suggested he should give up the car. She also pointed out that if what he said was true it would be folly for her to abandon a job that at least provided her with clothes and pocket-money. It's significant,' mused Mr Fogg, 'that she resolutely refused to contribute a penny of her earnings to the housekeeping expenses. They employed no servant and she kept the house, I suspect in a rather hugger-mugger fashion, in her spare time. Then the inevitable happened. She met a young man from London, who was staying with the Stocks on a visit, and fell passionately in love.'

'Probably have fallen in love with something out of the ape-house if it had worn the right clothes,' contributed Crook. 'What's she like by the way?'

'One of these days she will be a beauty,' replied Mr Fogg in decisive tones. 'At present—admittedly I didn't see her at her best—no one has taught her how to dress, what to do with her hands, how to make the best of herself in any way. But the promise is there and that, Crook, is one of the things that troubles me most. Ruth Garside is by no means the usual young woman, a bit awkward, a bit unpolished, but under the surface very much the same as every other girl of her age. She has immense capacities for feeling, she is, in short, a personality, and everything may, must, depend on the next few years. Such an ordeal as she has just passed through must leave its mark on the least receptive nature. My fear is that here it may wreck the rest of her life.'

'Let me tell you the next bit,' begged Crook. 'Daddy stepped in and wrecked the affair. How did he do it, by the way?'

'By a particularly mean trick. Really, when I think of that man, my blood boils. He agreed to invite this young fellow

—Blake was his name, Noel Blake, the only son of his mother and she a widow, all of which played a part in what followed —to his house. Blake came, expecting to find an ogre, and found instead a striking old fellow, with a head like a figure on a Roman coin, positively creamy with charm—it makes me squeamish to remember him in the witness-box, giving evidence against his own daughter—saying frankly that he wouldn't stand in the way of that daughter's happiness, but in fairness both to himself and the next generation, he thought there were certain facts the young man should know. He'd contrived to get the girl out of the room during this interview, of course. And then he told young Blake that the second Mrs Garside had died in an asylum—did I mention she had died some years before?—and he had, he regretted to admit, every reason to believe that the failing was congenital.'

'Slander,' commented Crook in crisp tones. 'Anything to back up the statement, d'you happen to know?'

'It is true that Mary Garside died in an institution; when her husband continued his refusal to give her a divorce, the inevitable happened. Her lover abandoned her—he was perfectly willing to marry her if Garside had made it possible—and she began to drift. She was about thirty at the time, certainly no more, and she still had some means, but these gradually became dissipated and unfortunately, as so many lonely and disappointed women do, she took to the bottle. She spent some time in an inebriates home as a voluntary patient, was discharged, made an attempt to rehabilitate herself, as they say nowadays, went back to the drink and, in short, there was a measure of truth in what Garside said.'

'About her, yes, but how about the girl?'

'There he had no justification, I feel convinced, for his assertions. He produced stray incidents, a fit of rage during which she threw a potted plant through a conservatory window, a tale of smashed china, once an ugly little affair of a kitchen knife thrown across the room, quite without effect. He forbore to add that the child was about nine years old at the time, and beside herself with passion because of some comment he had made about her mother.'

'He sounds a poor stick, young Blake,' said Crook dispassionately. 'All the same, it's not every young man who wants to take the contemporary version of Emily Brontë home to his doting mamma.'

'Oh, I don't fancy he was much of a loss,' Fogg agreed. 'It was the appalling consequences that trouble me. When she understood what her father had done, Ruth appears to have lost her head completely. She uttered the wildest threats, told him to his face she wished he were dead, said she wouldn't lift a finger to save him if she saw him in mortal danger—you can imagine it, perhaps. The unfortunate thing is that there was a witness to the scene in the person of a young fellow from the village, who was bringing up a weekly order of groceries.'

'I bet he didn't have to buy himself drinks for the following week,' murmured Crook, appreciatively. 'I must say, Fogg, your girl doesn't appear to do things by halves. How long before the alleged murder attempt?'

'Precisely a fortnight. Garside complained to his doctor, from whom he had various pills and potions in connection with his rotten heart (there was a violence in the older man's voice that brought Crook metaphorically to his feet), that his last bottle of medicine had produced symptoms consonant with some form of poisoning. The bottle was analysed and was found to contain a very small quantity of arsenic. It wasn't enough to prove fatal, in the doses prescribed on the bottle, but the fact remains there shouldn't have been any arsenic there.'

'And Garside suggested the girl had been dosing the stuff? Then why not give him enough to put him underground right away?"

'You have put your finger on the weakness of the Prosecution's case,' observed Fogg, with his wintry smile. 'It's a point the girl herself made. If I'd meant to poison him, she said, I wouldn't have stopped at half-measures. The doctor—not Stocks, you may be sure—was in a quandary. He had had a number of complaints recently and had reason to suppose his dispenser, a new man, tippled indiscreetly, and might perhaps be responsible. It wasn't a pleasant thought, but it was pleasanter than imagining the girl was trying to poison her own father. He took the bottle away and put up another himself; Garside ostentatiously kept this under lock and key and for about a month nothing more was heard of the charge. By this time father and daughter were no longer on speaking terms. Common sense would have dictated a separation, but under Miss Garside's will she had to remain with him until she was 21 unless she married.'

'Money is the root of all evil,' chanted Crook, softly.

'She was, not unnaturally, exceedingly bitter towards him by now, and had no intention of abdicating when in a few months, about a year, actually, she would come into her money and leave him for ever. She went on working for Stocks and he went on living much as he had done before. Then, about a month after the arsenic episode, Ruth found him one morning unconscious in his bed. She appears to have taken her time to call in medical help, in fact, she went to work as usual, only casually mentioning to Stocks in the course of the morning that she had left her father still asleep. Stocks, knowing he liked his little attentions, before his daughter left for her day's duties, was alarmed. He insisted on going to the cottage, where he found Andrew slowly coming round from an overdose of sleeping-mixture. That put the cat among the pigeons with a vengeance because this time the old man wasn't disposed to assume an accident. The remainder of the pills in the bottle were examined and it was found that a number, containing a high content of morphia, had been introduced among the quite harmless tablets the doctor had prescribed. There was no question now of inadvertence or accident, the thing was perfectly deliberate. Dr Fraser, the man's own doctor, couldn't shut his eyes to the possibilities. Everyone knew that Ruth had told her father she'd rejoice in his death, they reminded each other that she worked for a doctor, and Stocks, like a good many overworked country G.P.'s, had perhaps let her assume rather more responsibility than her age and experience warranted. Among other things she often delivered pills and mixtures to the owners of the outlying farms; it was simple to urge that she could substitute aspirin or something equally harmless for tablets containing drugs. Her father was supposed to take two tablets a night, two of *these* tablets would have proved fatal.'

'Then why wasn't he dead?' enquired Crook, sensibly.

'He had an answer to that. He said that as he was shaking

the tablets into the palm of his hand the previous night he dropped the phial, the tablets rolled in all directions, and so instead of taking the two top ones, as he would normally have done, he had taken one dangerous tablet and one harmless one. That, according to both doctors, would have precisely the result of keeping him unconscious for several hours longer than usual, without being fatal.'

'It don't sound to me according to Cocker,' said Crook, disbelieving. 'I mean, why upset the tablets that one night? Or was it a habit of his to roll them around his floor? No, no, Fogg, it's too damn' convenient. Do you mean to say he brought a case against the girl with no more to go on than that?'

'I think you under-estimate the gravity of the situation,' Fogg demurred. 'This was the second occasion when someone had tampered with his medicine. Fraser might find some excuse for the first, but not for the second. Somebody had introduced those alien tablets—there's no getting away from that.'

'So he goes to the police and brings a charge against his own daughter? Jam for you. Any reasonable jury would acquit her on that alone.' This was Crook at his most outrageous.

'No. No. He was far too clever for that. He didn't offer to prefer a charge, he just saw to it that the story went the rounds. How those pills got in among the rest when by rights there should have been none on the premises is a mystery to me, he'd say. And a good many fellows began to try and solve the mystery for themselves, and most of them came to the same conclusion. With only the two of them on the premises who but the girl could be responsible? And they'd just had that thundering row, they weren't on speaking terms—you can't live in a small community and hope to preserve any privacy. The next thing that happened was Stocks gave her notice. Not that he believed a word of it, so he says, but he's got his living to get like other men, and his patients began to drift away at an alarming rate. They didn't want their medicines put up by someone who might, just conceivably might, not be too scrupulous about what went into a bottle. The long and the short of it was, the gossip grew to such proportions that eventually the police stepped in, and Ruth Garside was arrested on a charge of attempted murder.'

'They had Glyn Roberts for the Prosecution, didn't they?' murmured Crook. 'A piece of cake for him.'

'I mentioned the Wallace case just now. It's apposite. Roberts made out a very strong case against the accused. She had had the run of the doctor's surgery, drugs were available, no one else had been inside the cottage, with the exception of young Blake, for several months, she was known to be on bad terms with the old man, they had their invaluable witness to what she'd said to him—which, incidentally, she didn't deny—by the time his last witness had sat down the case against Ruth Garside appeared to have been sewn up, as we say. And then it was the turn of the other side. Naturally, there was only one possible defence.'

'That the old man had done it himself?'

'Precisely. A very difficult defence to put over, incidentally. The question of motive arises at once, but to my mind that's pretty clear. Garside's an old man, older than he looks by several years; he's entirely dependent on his daughter. She's made no secret of the fact that the moment she comes of age she'll run out on him. He can starve for all she cares. He's scarcely likely to pick up another fortune at his age, and, under existing law, a child is no longer responsible for a parent's support. So, his one chance is by hook or crook to retain control of the money. If the girl is either in prison or in some institution for the feeble-minded the handling of the income will stay with him. He has a little foundation to build on with his story of the mother, so if he can persuade the authorities that the girl really should not be at large . . .'

'Bob's your uncle,' agreed Crook. 'Bit far-fetched, ain't it?' He looked dubious.

'I told you it was very difficult to—er—swing, as you would say. But no other defence was possible. And when you come to examine means, motive and opportunity you'll find that Andrew Garside has as much of all three as had the girl. You know these ramshackle old country places, I dare say. Ah well!' as Crook shook a decisive head—it took a case to drag him out of London— 'There are outhouses, tumbledown barns, sheds, and we proved that there was a partly-used tin of weedkiller available, as there so often is. Neither Miss Garside nor her father was a gardener, but the tin had been kept closed and the poison was still fit for use. Moreover, we brought an expert into the court to show that the tin had recently been opened. Unfortunately it proved impossible to obtain any reputable fingerprints, but the girl swore she never visited the shed, and the prosecution were unable to produce a witness to refute her statement. No one else, except the old man, had access to the stuff, and though we were equally unable to offer proof, we relied on getting the benefit of the doubt. Glyn Roberts returned to the point again and again, but he was unable to shake my client. She told the jury she never worked in the garden, and certainly the state of the garden bore out her assertion. He wrapped up the question in half a dozen different ways, but always with the same result. Garside must have had the wit to know that a small dose of arsenic is unlikely to be fatal, I don't doubt he checked his facts and knew precisely how much would be safe. It's a point in the accused's favour that the amount in the bottle could scarcely have killed him if he had taken the entire supply in one draught.'

'Your argument bein' that if she meant to put out Dad's light she wouldn't stop at any half-way house.'

'The young lady made the position perfectly clear. Why should I arouse suspicion by giving him enough to make him suspicious of me but not enough to secure my own freedom? she demanded. Glyn Roberts's reply was that she hoped Garside would feel so unsafe that he would let her go, taking the money with her, to which Ruth Garside replied, that only shows how little you know my father. I'm by no means certain,' added Mr Fogg, primly, 'that the spectacle of a father and daughter in mutual accusation is not more deplorable than a similar situation between husband and wife.'

'I've never been so hearty myself on the one about blood bein' thicker than water,' murmured Crook. 'Disillusionin' profession, ours, ain't it?'

Mr Fogg let that pass. 'The Prosecution had established motive,' he continued in his sedate fashion. 'We offered means and opportunity.'

'The first time,' Crook agreed. 'How about the pills?'

'These proved more difficult, but after a good deal of research we were able to trace the district nurse who had assisted during Miss Garside's last illness. The doctor, unhappily, had died the previous year and his records were not available. This woman declared that she recalled the case very well, because she had been shocked that a girl of 15 should be allowed to shoulder so much responsibility. She appears to be one of the few women upon whom Andrew Garside was unable to impose his treacherous charm. She remembered that pills containing morphia had been prescribed, and said that, the cottage being very remotely situated, and the doctor realising there was little he could do beyond minimising the patient's suffering by the use of drugs, a supply rather larger than was normal had been left at the house. The girl had been told in no circumstances to exceed the prescribed dose, which was one tablet at a time. Two tablets would be fatal. The nurse couldn't say with any assurance if any tablets had remained after Miss Garside's death and, if so, whether they had been disposed of. Garside himself disclaimed all knowledge of sick-room etiquette, explaining that illness distressed him too much for him to play any active part in the care for his sister—that statement, incidentally, did us as much good as any evidence we could offer —and he had no idea what happened to the pills and potions after his sister's death.'

'If he'd been my client,' observed Crook, 'he'd have definitely remembered handin' them back to the doctor, or seein' them destroyed.'

'I doubt whether that would have helped him much,' returned Mr Fogg in severe tones. 'He could hardly have hoped to prove that he had not examined the contents of the boxes, bottles, et cetera and he would have admitted knowledge of the nature of the tablets. Besides the nurse could have testified that he absented himself from the sick-room on every occasion —I believe he was actually out of the house at the time of the poor lady's death—no, he was probably well advised to stick to his story . . .'

'Which may, of course, have been true.'

'It is naturally my contention that it was false, that he came upon these tablets and saw another opportunity of pressing his case against this unfortunate girl. And I fancy the jury thought it a rather odd coincidence that for the second time the dose should be insufficient to cause death. Mind you, they were grievously exercised in their minds. They were out for four hours, and their verdict certainly amounted to no more than Not Proven. And it is that, Crook, which lies so heavily on my mind. Miss Garside may be under the impression that she has been found innocent, whereas that is certainly not the case.'

'You're not suggestin' you left any stones unturned?' cried his companion. 'Come to that, I don't think old Garside's position's an enviable one.'

A grimly malicious smile crossed the K.C.'s face. 'If it is true, what I have urged in court, that he was the responsible agent, he must feel woefully duped,' he said. 'As soon as the result of the trial was known Dick Devenish approached him to say that he proposed to remove the girl from her father's jurisdiction—care is really not the word—and to accept responsibility for her until she came of age. This would involve taking control of her income until that time.'

'Did the old boy agree?' asked Crook.

'Devenish gave him no choice. He intimated that, should Garside refuse, he would advise Ruth to bring a counter-charge . . . He climbed down at once, adding a little late in the day that he would never feel safe with his daughter under his roof.'

'He has my sympathy there,' said Crook heartily. 'Lucrezia Borgia wouldn't be my cup of tea either. Besides, it 'ud be throwin' in the sponge to have her back, put ideas in folks' minds. I mean, and in most cases there's plenty of room for 'em. Come now, Fogg, what's eatin' you? You've got the girl off, you've got her away from Papa, in a year's time she'll be an heiress . . .'

'My fear,' said Mr Fogg, 'is that all her life she will labour under the disadvantage of an appalling suspicion. But—it's more than that. Have you never come across people who appear to be singled out by fate for misfortune? Hotels in which they stay catch fire, ships on which they sail sink, trains they board are involved in accidents. It's as though for them

16

Fate throws with a loaded dice, tosses with a two-headed penny . . .'

'And you think this girl's one of those?'

'I can't forget her face and the sense of—of impending doom with which I was overwhelmed in her presence. If ever she should find herself involved in another tragedy, she'll start under such a burden of prejudice that the fight will be half lost before it has begun, and I cannot rid myself of a sense of failure. If only I could have proved her innocence. To be convinced of it, as I am, as I do, is not enough. And I cannot believe that a young woman of her spirit and appearance is going to sink into obscurity. I have what you, my dear fellow, would call a hunch about her future. The next time the limelight plays upon her the result may well depend on what took place in that court last week. I have been back in London for several days, and I have, naturally, other cases in hand, but I can't forget her, Crook. One day I am convinced we shall hear of Miss Garside again.'

2

It was more than five years before Crook had any reason to recall this conversation. One winter evening in 1953 he called in at the Blue Bottle on his way back from Bloomsbury Street, where he worked, *en route* for Brandon Street, where he lived. Sitting in a corner of the bar was a young man whom he had encountered casually in the same surroundings on a number of occasions, and with whom, in his normal garrulous fashion, he had got into conversation. The young fellow was sitting alone, looking pretty glum, and Crook, who had no inhibitions about not being wanted, carried his own beer over to join him.

'Hallo!' said the man, whose name was Frank Hardy, 'you're the very chap I wanted to see. It must be telepathy.'

'Or just coincidence,' Crook grinned. 'In a spot? Then you couldn't come to a better address. My clients are always innocent . . .'

'It's not precisely that kind of a spot,' said Frank. 'It's just —well, actually I'd be glad of your advice. You remember I went abroad in the spring.'

'On the Continong,' agreed Crook. He thought himself it was an odd predilection, but one shared by thousands of his fellow-countrymen. For himself, he hadn't left his native land since returning to it with the utmost despatch in 1919, after three years of dodging German bullets and shells, and he was inclined to remark that foreign parts were too damn' dangerous for a chap who hoped to die in his own bed.

'Just before I came back,' Frank Hardy continued, 'I was involved in a vague sort of way in an affair that struck me as being pretty rum at the time, and that still gives me the same impression. I thought it was just one of those things, and when I got back I put it out of my mind . . .'

'And now,' suggested Crook amiably, 'you're discovering that old sins have long shadows.'

The young man started. 'What made you say that?'

'You can't see your own face in the glass,' said Crook. 'Besides you wouldn't be coming to me for advice about a bit of romantic nonsense. That ain't up my street at all. What's the trouble? A lady in the case?'

'Yes,' agreed Frank, 'but not quite as you imagine. Listen. I was walking along the Corniche Road one afternoon when I noticed a huge white car, a Broadbent, flying past in a manner that suggested it was being driven by a lunatic.'

'Woman driver?' enquired Crook ungallantly. 'Think nothing of it. Probably late for an appointment with her hairdresser. Well, she didn't turn over or anything, did she?'

'No. Though I must admit I expected to come upon the wreckage every time I turned a corner. When I got into Ventimiglia the car was drawn up by the coast road near the flower market, and her driver had the bonnet up. I went over to know if I could do anything. The woman turned and looked at me as if she didn't see I was there, right through me, Crook. It gave me the creeps. When I asked the second time she said no, it was all right, she was knocking a bit—an understatement if ever I heard one—but she'd been driving her rather hard. Her husband was waiting to take the car out to an important appointment, and she was late already. I gathered he wouldn't be too pleased. I said, reasonably enough, that if the car wasn't safe she'd better leave it at a garage, and she sort of laughed and said that wouldn't be necessary, her husband was a first-class mechanic, and she'd warn him she wasn't running true, and if he thought her unsafe he could ring up a local garage and get a car from there. I said anyway she'd better let the car cool down a bit, so she pulled out a cigarette case, a very fancy affair, with R.A. on it in diamonds. She told me her husband was an agent for a thing called Motors Inc. Know it?'

'You want the unattainable, we can get it for you—at a price,' returned Crook dryly. 'Yes, I know it. I bet the police do, too.'

'He was on the Continent selling Broadbents, among other

things,' Frank Hardy continued. 'He'd had a date for that afternoon and wanted the car. That caused a bit of a scrimmage because she'd promised to take a sick kid and her mother into Mentone to some famous clinic there. The kid was motorshy and couldn't go in on the coach—they have damn' fine coaches on that road—and Mrs Appleyard (I learnt her name later)—had promised to drive them in. Appleyard eventually agreed to postpone his engagement, and off she went directly after lunch. They were staying at a villa, by the way, just behind Bordighera.'

'She seems to have been remarkably confidin' to a casual acquaintance,' suggested Crook.

'I didn't pick all that up at the time, a lot of it came later. She did tell me about the muddle over the car, and when I suggested again she should leave her at a garage she said no, because her husband would probably want to show its paces, and off she drove very carefully, too carefully for an experienced driver, as she obviously was.'

'Sober?' murmured Crook.

'As a judge. My impression was she'd had some appalling shock, taken the knock one hundred per cent and if her guardian angel hadn't been on point duty that afternoon she'd never have got home in one piece.'

'Any idea of the nature of the shock?'

'Only my own conjectures, but see how it appears to you. She was the sort of woman it would be difficult to forget, a real beauty—you never saw such eyes, a deep dark blue like an Italian sea when the shadows are going over it. She was dressed like a fashion-plate, and it was easy to see she took her clothes as much for granted as she took the gold cigarette-case and the crocodile bag she carried, and that cost every penny of fifty pounds or I'm a Dutchman—and, as you know, my home's in Canada. And a Broadbent isn't a poor man's car. One way and another, they run into the five-to-six thousand mark.'

'Beats me how any honest man can afford to run a car like that these days,' remarked Crook, simply. 'But maybe that ain't a consideration that troubles Appleyard. Well?'

'I saw her out of sight and then I went along and got myself fixed up with a room. But I couldn't get her out of my mind.

The next day I walked along the coast into Bordighera—I was staying in Ventimiglia for two or three days—and I stopped for a drink at the Garibaldi Hotel. It was out of season, and there were very few tourists, and only two English guests, an old couple who'd lived on the Riviera for the past thirty years, till the war drove them out of their villa at Mentone, and who had settled down at the Garibaldi for the rest of their natural lives. The old boy was a handsome bag of bones, rising eighty and rather deaf. His wife was a bit younger, with English-woman stamped all over her. I dare say I shouldn't have noticed them particularly, if it hadn't been for overhearing a scrap of their conversation. You know how it is when a hotel's more than half-empty, particularly abroad. The chap who brings your drink generally stops for a chat, particularly if you're British. They like to practise their English on you. This chap put my drink down without a word and went off to the old couple in the corner. They were all talking English and I heard the word accident, and then something about poor Ruth Appleyard, it's terrible. That made me sit up. Mind you, I didn't know her name then, but the initials on the cigarette-case had been R.A. Just coincidence perhaps but—well, I listened in. It was the old boy who put me on the track. Speaking in that high fluting voice you often get with old men who're also deaf, he said, "What on earth did the feller expect? You can't take cars like that vulgar white monstrosity up the mountain roads at 80." And something about horses being good enough when he was a young man. That was enough for me. As soon as the waiter had moved off I moved in. I asked them if by any chance they had an English paper, that's always a safe opening. Apparently they had but it was upstairs in their private sitting-room. I said no matter, and brought the conversation round to the accident, explaining that I'd seen a white Broadbent in trouble the night before. I wanted the driver to take it into a garage, I said. Did it crash on the way back? Then I got my real shock because, as perhaps you've realised, it wasn't Mrs A. who had crashed but her husband. "He was always reckless," sighed old Mrs Arkwright. "Criminal", muttered the old boy. "Takin' risks like that for a little slut." That's where I began to put two and two together.'

21

'And make it about 96, I dare say. What have you got, anyway? Girl tells her husband the car's missing a bit, he decides it's O.K. and goes off, takes the one chance too many, and loses out.'

'If it was that way,' agreed Frank, slowly. 'Only you see, it wasn't.'

'Meaning?' Crook was as alert as a dog watching the approach of an enemy.

'Meaning she didn't tell him.'

There was a brief pause while Crook had their glasses refilled. Then he asked, 'Who says she didn't?'

'She does. Listen. There was an inquest, of course, and I went to it. Old Mrs Arkwright wanted to come, but her husband dissuaded her. "Dear Ruth ought to have another woman there," she kept saying. It must be such a ghastly shock in fact, two, one after the other, her husband's death and learning about the girl—the little slut old Arkwright had referred to. Because—and this is the point, Crook—she was absolutely convinced she knew nothing about another woman.'

'And you're convinced she did?'

'I can't forget that shocked look she was wearing the first time I met her, that look of someone who's recently heard something too bad to be true. There was another bit of evidence that came out later. An American called Winslow was driving up from the coast past the villa early that afternoon, and he noticed a big white car parked round the corner just below the villa but out of sight of it. A woman was at the wheel, crouched over it; he thought she was ill, and was just going to stop when suddenly she threw a lighted cigarette through the window and went down the road like a bat out of hell. He said he thought she must be crazy. There's no doubt at all it was Mrs Appleyard. Crook, how does that work out? At the inquest she said she found she had time to spare so stopped for a cigarette, knowing she wouldn't be able to smoke once she'd collected the mother and the kid. It doesn't make sense. If you've got time to spare you smoke your cigarette at home, or at any rate halfway, you don't pull up just out of sight of the windows. This fellow said the same as I did—she looked shocked to death. I'll swear she'd just learned something that knocked her off her pins. It would be so simple. Her husband had said he'd ring up this contact and postpone the appointment. Say she goes back for something she's forgotten. He's telephoning. I've seen the place. You go up some steps from the road into a small garden; the window of the sitting-room would be wide open, the telephone's in that room, it was a scorching day, a voice would carry for miles. He thinks she's safely out of the way, he's explaining why he'll be late. Wouldn't that fit the bill?'

'Sure,' agreed Crook. 'What's her story?'

'About the car? Oh, she says she brought it back, travelling very carefully, and left it in front of the villa. She went up the steps and into the house to warn her husband it wasn't safe to drive—she told the story about the engine knocking—but he'd gone. She looked for him in every room in the house, in the garden, everywhere. She supposed he'd got tired of waiting and telephoned the garage. There wasn't a note or anything, but I gather he wasn't much of a correspondent. She said she was exhausted and very hot, so she went into the bathroom and took a bath. Then she mixed herself a drink, and it was only then she remembered she'd left the car unlocked in the road. She thought she might as well put it in the garage, and get it attended to next day. When she went down to the gate she found to her amazement the car had disappeared. She swore it didn't occur to her that her husband might have taken it, she was so sure he wasn't in the villa on her return. There had been some local cases of joy-riding, the "borrowed" cars being found casually abandoned by the roadside. She was alarmed because the car was unreliable. She went a little distance down the road in case it had escaped and run backwards, though, as the villa was on a slope, she'd left it in gear. She came back and after a little while telephoned the police. They asked her if she was sure her husband hadn't taken it, and she said yes she was sure, but she would telephone the garage to confirm this.'

'And the garage,' chipped in Crook, 'said they hadn't heard anything from Mr A.'

'Precisely. That was when she began to get the wind up. She told the court she couldn't understand how he could have gone off without her knowing. She did suggest that she was in the bathroom with the tap running, so perhaps he called out and she didn't hear, but dash it all, Crook, they were married folk, surely he could have pushed open the door and stuck his head in.'

'What's your idea then?'

'What proof is there that he wasn't at home when she came in and she didn't tell him about the car?'

'Sent him to his death for the sake of a little slut who probably didn't amount to sixpence anyway? I know dames are crazy, but I doubt if they're as crazy as that. Didn't you say the old lady spoke of her bein' devoted to the husband?'

'Don't you see, that would make it worse? I tell you, when I saw her she was—distraught. She'd recently undergone some frightful shock. And from what I could learn she'd never had the smallest suspicion that he was being unfaithful.'

'What did she say about that at the inquest or didn't it arise?'

'She said her husband hadn't told her the nature of the engagement, but she assumed it was to do with the sale of a Broadbent. She stuck to that in spite of all the questions, and there were a good many. They couldn't shake her.'

'Find out anything else? Any family or anything?'

'Apparently none. My informant was Mrs Arkwright, who seemed to have got to know them fairly well. Appleyard went out first, and it was while he was alone there that he got entangled with this girl. Then Mrs Appleyard followed, and they moved to the villa. They seemed to have lived a kind of dream-life, dancing, gambling, travelling—how they did it on the currency allowance, search me. I doubt if they'd ever heard of economy. Even in London they seemed to live in the best hotels. It was quite late that evening that a lorry driver reported seeing the wreck of a car at the foot of one of the mountain roads. It was a solitary place, miles from any dwelling. A man could have lain there some hours without being found. The car was a twisted mass of metal, with nothing to indicate the condition it had been in when it had left the road. The driver, of course, was as dead as a door-nail.'

'Open verdict?' murmured Crook.

The young man shrugged. 'Anything else was out of the question. It could have happened the way she said. At all events, no one will ever be able to prove that it didn't.'

'Or, what may be equally important, that it did. Y'know, something strikes me as queer. Why tell such an improbable story if it wasn't true? Why not say, "I warned him about the car. He tinkered with it and said it was all right," or wouldn't listen to me? Why spring this incredible story about being invisible, and suddenly reappearing and going off without a word? Was he fond of walking?'

'Walking?' Frank stared. 'I shouldn't think so. Owners of Broadbents seldom are. That was another point—where was he when she arrived at the villa? It was a scorching afternoon, as I said—did he go for a stroll to pass the time or what?'

'Or what,' repeated Crook. 'Your guess is as good as mine. It's such a rum story it could be true. Anyhow, it's not our affair.'

'Not yours perhaps,' Frank Hardy agreed.

'Eh? What's your interest?'

'Let's have some more beer,' suggested Frank, irrelevantly, 'Crook, don't they say there's a pattern in life?'

'Some chaps do,' Crook allowed, 'but you'd need to be a corkscrew to trace it.'

'Then listen to this. When I came over from Canada I was under instructions to dig up a cousin of mine, some degrees removed, but still—a relation. She's a woman in the early forties, married to a chap called Dingle, a barrister living in the north. I went up for a week-end a fortnight ago, and hinted pretty broadly that I wouldn't refuse an invitation for Christmas. She looked a bit bothered, then explained she and her husband always went south to stay with her mother-in-law, an old trout called Lady Dingle. If I didn't mind . . . I said it was if Lady Dingle didn't mind, and she laughed in rather an odd way and said, oh, she won't object, she has a penchant for young men, and apparently lately she's extended it to young women. She's got a new companion-chauffeuse, a Mrs Appleyard, who seems to have swept the board, according to Kate. Kate, she told me, had been with the family thirty years, starting as governess to Isobel Dingle, Lady D's only daughter, and stopping on as housekeeper and general dogsbody when the girl left home.'

'Any proof it's the same Mrs Appleyard? It's not such an uncommon name,' Crook urged.

'I asked what Dorothy knew about her. She said, "Oh, she's a widow, her husband was killed in a motoring accident on the Continent about two months ago. She seems to have dug herself in very comfortably. Apparently she was left very badly off when her husband died, and had to take any job that offered. Kate has warned us we may all find our noses put out of joint by her." Lady D.'s a very rich woman,' added Frank abruptly. 'Mrs Appleyard has practically talked the old lady into buying a new car, she's treated more like a daughter than a paid companion . . . I don't like it, Crook. Suppose there's an accident down at Dingle Hall when they're out driving, say?'

'Mrs Appleyard loses a job,' returned Crook in crisp tones. 'Now, my dear chap, pull yourself together. You don't even know this is the same woman. Even if it is, what could you say of her? That she didn't prevent her husband crashing over a mountainous road in an unseaworthy car. There's such a thing as slander, and you'd do well to avoid it. Still—you say you're going down for Christmas?'

'Yes.'

'So you'll soon know if it's the same one. If there was anything fishy about the inquest, you won't see her for dust. If she brazens it out—well, she'll recognise you, I suppose, and that'll make her put the brake on—if she was planning anything, that is. By the way, you didn't happen to learn her maiden name?'

'After I heard Dorothy's news, I went along to Somerset House and checked the marriage. It occurred to me there might have been a previous husband who came to a sticky end. She was Ruth Garside. Why, does that mean anything to you?'

Crook said it did, and explained why.

3

When Ruth Garside fell in love with Jack Appleyard, Mrs Martin, in whose house she was boarding at the time, moved heaven and earth to try and prevent the marriage.

'He's a gold-digger, a fortune-hunter,' she warned her brother, Richard Devenish. 'He's after her money. If she lost that she'd never set eyes on Master Jack again. I doubt if he's ever done an honest day's work in his life. They had a name for young men like that when I was a girl. We called them gigolos. She mustn't be allowed to do it, Dick. She's had trouble enough as it is.'

But it would have taken a great deal more than the combined efforts of Mrs Martin and her brother to stop Ruth. She was over the moon with love, couldn't imagine how she had ever considered marrying a pale young dreamer like Noel Blake. Half the girls she knew were in love with Jack. Against everyone's advice they married, and, to everyone's amazement, the marriage worked. Ruth's beauty, prophesied by old Thomas Fogg, bloomed overnight. She was so radiant, heads turned everywhere she went. She and Jack made a wonderful couple. He was a gambler to his fingertips, and it was nothing to her that he should gamble with her money.

'It'll be the first time it's brought anyone any happiness,' she declared.

During the four years of their marriage they never had any settled abode.

'We can settle down when we're old,' he used to coax her. 'In the meantime, life is for living.'

And how they lived. They seemed to take the sunshine with them. Jack had a theory that you must have the best because it is the best. 'Money begets money,' he said. 'If we live in Pimlico and you shop in Kensington High Street we'll never get anywhere.' At the end of a year you wouldn't have recognised the stubborn, sullen Ruth who had come south, in the glittering, gloriously happy creature who flashed, with her husband, from Paris to Monte Carlo and from Monte Carlo to Rome. To the end of his life she was never sure how her husband made his living—a commission agent, darling, he'd say airily. Certainly he had the faculty of making two pounds grow where one had grown before, and he saw to it that the Chancellor of the Exchequer never laid any hands on his profits. Ruth was beautifully dressed and, after her marriage, never went in public transport unless Jack happened to be abroad 'clinching a big thing, darling, you'd be bored to tears, and I wouldn't have a minute to take you around.' After his death her life seemed to collapse about her. The odd thing was that, though Jack hadn't been a good man, not honest or true, a bit of a twister, not even dependable, he had possessed some gift that can't be acquired by men who have all the virtues. He was like a gardener who has green fingers. He may beat his wife and drink his wages, while his children go barefoot, but wherever he labours, flowers grow. Jack had had green fingers for life; pessimists saw a rift in the clouds, disappointed men realised there's always tomorrow; sad men heard his infectious laugh and were surprised at their own melancholy.

Ruth learned quite a little about his sidelines when she was forced to go through his papers, understood that the little slut hadn't been the first of his infidelities. When she had discovered her existence on that last appalling afternoon, running back to the villa, just as Frank Hardy had foreseen, and hearing Jack talking in that warm creamy voice—'of course I'm coming, darling, you know what they say about joy deferred, yes, I swear—what's that? oh, come, darling, I always warned you I was an old married man—' it was as if her heart died in her breast with such an access of pain that she could only run the car to the corner and sit there, smoking, stabbed with incredulous agony. It was a very hot day; you could almost hear the dragon-flies darting in the sun, but Ruth didn't hear them, she heard only the voice of Jack, her lover, her husband, her loyal friend, she'd thought, talking to another woman in the voice she had believed he kept only for her. She hadn't even noticed the big Buick and its driver, had realised only that some spring of life in her was broken and she didn't know how it would ever be mended.

At the inquest she told her story without faltering and with a vehemence no one could shake. She had no lawyer to defend her, no lawyer, she asserted, could change the truth. After the verdict of death by misadventure, Lois Wheeler, whose child she had driven into Mentone on that fatal afternoon, came over to say quite calmly, 'Congrats, darling. At one minute I thought you weren't going to be able to swing it.'

Ruth turned. 'Does that mean you don't believe the evidence?'

Lois's long green eyes shone with a secret amusement. 'Hell, darling,' she protested. 'There wasn't any. Just your story. Jack couldn't tell his.'

'And you think it isn't true?'

There was something rather frightening about Ruth. Prudently Lois drew in her horns.

'I never said that, darling, of course I didn't. All I meant was I was afraid you might not be able to persuade the jury. Still, Jack only got what was coming to him. This should be a lesson to husbands. Men are bastards, all of 'em.'

'What you've just said is actionable,' Ruth was shaking, her eyes blazed. 'Yes, of course it is. A lawyer once told me, when you've been found innocent . . .'

'Found innocent? Ruth, darling, what are you talking about? No one ever suggested—Ruth, what lawyer was that? You didn't have one—this time. Tell me.' Her voice sank. 'Was Jack Appleyard your first husband?'

'Of course. What you're trying to say is that I've lied, that I deliberately let Jack go to his death because I knew . . . I knew . . .'

'But, darling, you told the court you didn't know.'

'No one can prove anything, they'll never be able to prove anything. It was accidental death, the jury agreed.'

Lois nodded. 'Yes, darling. It was accidental death. Bad luck for Jack.'

After Lois had gone and Ruth was back in the room she had shared with her husband, she remembered Thomas Fogg's clear unemotional voice saying, 'No, Miss Garside. You have not been found innocent. You have been found not guilty. There's a world of difference.'

'There was no proof,' she stammered then, as she had cried again today. 'No proof.'

And so, because of this absence of proof, she had escaped the net for the second time. That's what people would say; she would be regarded as one of the lucky ones, because there was no proof.

4

Miss Shaw-Benson, proprietor of the At Your Service Agency, was a viper of a woman, dressed in well-cut suits, whose advertisements declared that she could meet your every need. Nothing too large, nothing too small. Her fees were outrageous and she demanded outsize wages for her staff, but her reputation was such that she never lacked for clients. When Ruth Appleyard, recommended by Mrs Martin's daughter, Audrey, came into her office to register for work, she saw at once that she had got here something quite out of the ordinary. She asked Ruth the usual questions but was aware that the answers she received were by no means the whole story. There was a mystery here, she thought. A woman who could afford to apply for a job, wearing a Lachasse suit, had some story behind her.

'Where have you been employed up till now?' she said.

'I haven't worked since my marriage, when I was 21. My husband was recently killed in an accident, and I have to earn my living.'

'Had you given any thought to qualifications?'

Ruth had wondered, vaguely, if she couldn't sell hats—in Bond Street, of course. Miss Shaw-Benson pointed out briskly that she would need either capital or the ability to introduce a substantial body of new clients. Ruth, it appeared, had travelled most of her married life, she had no 'set' in the fashionable world.

'Then that's out. What else can you do?'

Ruth thought she could run a bridge club, she was a good player and she and Jack had sometimes given bridge lessons when other things weren't paying their way.

'Giving lessons won't get you far, unless you've some capital, and some connections,' the alarming woman assured her. ' Assuming, as I do, that you mean a bona-fide bridge club. I'm not interested in the other sort.'

It appeared that all Ruth's capabilities belonged to the luxury class. She couldn't do shorthand or book-keeping, she couldn't train children, and she obviously wouldn't last long serving behind a counter.

'I could be a doctor's receptionist,' suggested Ruth.

'Not if the doctor was married,' reflected Miss Shaw-Benson grimly.

She wondered what Ruth's story really was. In any case, she didn't imagine the girl would need to earn her living for long. Either she would marry again or acquire a wealthy protector.

'I've nothing on my books at the moment that would suit you,' she said. 'Where are you staying?'

Ruth was staying with Mrs Martin, which sounded respectable enough.

'Call in again next week,' advised Miss Shaw-Benson.

She never expected to see Ruth again, but two days later the girl reappeared. After that she called every morning for ten days. Miss Shaw-Benson began to feel her reputation for fitting the round peg into the round hole was at stake, so when Cecil Dingle blew into the office she regarded him as an answer to a prayer.

Cecil was the younger son of a formidable old woman who, under an infamous will, had been given sole control of a considerable fortune. She had a passion for power and lost no opportunity of exercising it. Cecil was forty-seven at the time, tall, thin, anxious-looking, and he stormed into the office wearing that air of resolution only achieved by normally timid men who suddenly find themselves fighting for existence in the last ditch.

'I'm looking for a companion for my mother,' he announced, as if he were buying a saucepan. 'I should warn you straight away that she's a tough proposition, so it's no use offering someone who'll crumple up or weep the first time my mother barks at her.'

It was not easy to discompose Miss Shaw-Benson.

'Does she bite as well?' she asked, coolly.

'That would depend on the companion. I can tell you this, she'd appreciate one who bit back.'

Miss Shaw-Benson displayed a degree of affability that would have staggered her staff. No one knew how bored she was by the routine employer, and here apparently was someone not afraid to speak his mind. Here also, though she didn't say so at once, might be a possible employer for the difficult but intriguing Mrs Appleyard.

'What qualifications does your mother expect?' she wanted to know.

Cecil rattled off a list as glibly as if he'd been rehearsing them all the way up from Dingle Halt, as indeed he had.

'She must be a reliable car-driver, with a clean licence; she should play a reasonable hand of bridge and be able to keep up with my mother's conversation. There's no question of a 44-hour week or what my mother would call nonsense of that sort at Dingle Hall. And if she can read French with a passable accent, that would be a great advantage.' He stopped, out of breath at his own courage. Miss Shaw-Benson admired it, too, though she didn't say so.

'Presumably Lady Dingle realises the market value of these remarkable qualifications,' she suggested, not of course believing it for a moment. It was her experience that the more people asked the less they expected to pay. She was always waiting for the would-be employer who anticipated a fee for the advantage of her company. 'What salary had you in mind?'

When she heard Lady Dingle's usual figure she tossed the form into the waste-paper basket.

'I hope you didn't make the journey simply on this account,' she said. 'It would have been cheaper and much less trouble for you to telephone.'

'Look here,' said Cecil, white with anxiety. 'I've got to get someone right away. Never mind about the salary. I'll juggle that somehow if you've got the right person.'

'I have one client on my books who might suit,' Miss Shaw-Benson acknowledged. 'She has all the qualifications and she's young enough to stand up to difficulties. Of course,' she added carelessly, 'your mother may prefer elderly women. They're more in her tradition. Mrs Appleyard is twenty-five, a widow without children.'

'My mother certainly wouldn't mind her being young,' said

Cecil eagerly. 'She always complains she only gets the throw-outs.'

'What else does she expect?' asked his companion coolly. 'If you're only prepared to pay bargain basement prices, you can't expect top-class goods. Tell me a little more about the post, Mr Dingle. Would Mrs Appleyard have any company besides your mother?'

Cecil thought it was a good thing Lady Dingle couldn't hear that; she'd probably have thrown up her hands, had a heart attack, and passed out on the spot.

'There's Kate Waring; she was governess to my sister as a child, and she's stayed with us ever since.'

'So she'd hardly be Mrs Appleyard's contemporary. Is there any younger companionship for her? I don't like to recommend someone who won't be able to stay the course, and, as you'll appreciate, I owe responsibility to both sides.'

'There's the bridge-playing community,' Cecil sounded a little doubtful. 'They come in all shapes and sizes. I don't mix with them much myself, but we have a perfect zoo of players in the neighbourhood. They're always on the look-out for a new-comer. But, if you mean will she get a chance to go dancing and so forth, no, I should think not. If you want that sort of fun, you have to go to the towns, or so Violet, my fiancée, tells me.'

The mention of Violet brought the further confession that he was in a particular hurry to make some adequate arrange-ment for Lady Dingle, because he was himself proposing to be married the following week.

'Everything was lined up,' he said. 'We had had a Miss Bennett for about eight months and suddenly there was a flare-up, I don't know the ins and outs of it ('But you could guess them,' reflected Miss Shaw-Benson shrewdly. 'Your precious Mamma is probably the original Mrs Dracula.'). Anyway, Miss Bennett packed her bags and was off in four and twenty hours.'

'That still leaves the ex-governess,' Miss Shaw-Benson sug-gested.

'She can't drive—or play bridge—or read French.'

'And, of course, dear Mamma would sooner see your mar-

riage broken off than go without her amenities for a fortnight,'
reflected Miss Shaw-Benson. And that was about the size of it.
Lady Dingle, having kept her son a bachelor for so long,
wasn't minded to lose him now. Well, it made a change from
the usual spinster daughter with the worm feeding on her
damask cheek.

'I'll ring up Mrs Appleyard. Where would you like to see
her? As a matter of fact, she'll probably be in soon.'

Cecil, however, longed only to be away from this pre-
dominantly feminine atmosphere. 'Could she come to the
Countryman's Club?' he asked, giving the address. Miss Shaw-
Benson got a few more details from him and rang up Ruth.

'She's a vampire—no doubt about that—but if you can
stand up to her it might suit you,' she said. 'At least you won't
have to walk a poodle in the park or go shopping in the Knights-
bridge stores.'

Violet Ross was a farmer's daughter, who had learned shorthand and typing and got a job on the Dingle estate of which
Cecil was manager. She had been appointed as his secretary
after six months, and within a year he discovered he couldn't
do without her, and not merely in the office. Haggard and
desperate, he proposed, and to his amazement, for he was inclined to believe his mother's estimate of him, was accepted.

'Doing well for yourself, Vi,' said her sister, Ethel, herself
married to a young farmer in the neighbourhood.

'If you call having a scorpion for your mother-in-law doing
well, then I'm tops,' said Violet calmly. 'Know what, Ethel?
It's not the murders that are done that surprise me, it's the
ones that aren't. Old Lady D., rot her, has just lived in Cecil's
life like an aphis fly in the body of the living wasp. She broke
up one marriage for him long ago—no, he didn't tell me in so
many words, but it leaked out, without him so much as knowing he'd told me. I can't think,' she went on in reflective tones,
'why we only hang people who commit actual physical murder.
Surely the murder of the spirit is a much worse crime.'

'Couldn't he have got away from her?' asked Ethel, who
wasn't at all sure she liked Vi marrying a man more than
twenty years her senior.

'There's the estate. Someone has to look after that, and Roger, the elder son, always wanted to go in for the law and his father liked the idea. That only left Cecil. Anyway, Roger doesn't give a row of beans for it. If you ask me, the old witch's favourite child is Isobel. *She* just walked out on her twenty-first birthday—and went up to London and got a job. She was married and expecting her first baby before she saw her mother again. If only Cecil had had the guts—but he's got too much imagination. He sees her cast in his mould—kind and feeling hurt. All nonsense. You could just as easily hurt a bronze Buddha.'

'What's she like to you?' enquired Ethel.

'Civil but only just. She still thinks she can break it up. Well, she's got a shock coming. She can't, but that won't stop her trying.'

Violet, the merciless representative of the merciless young, was quite right. On the eve of the marriage the old woman contrived to reduce her companion to hysterics and to pack her off next morning. She then sent for her son and insisted on another companion being produced instantly.

'Well, really, Mamma,' protested Cecil. 'We're getting married on Thursday week.'

'I suppose in an emergency like this'—her voice was like ice—'you could even postpone your wedding, having waited so long.'

'It wouldn't be any good,' said Cecil. 'Vi's made up her mind. She'd come round here bag and baggage.'

'I simply cannot conceive'—Lady Dingle shuddered—'how any parents of sensibility could have given that girl the name of Violet. Tiger-Lily would be better. Still, I suppose even she will have the decency to realise you can't go gallivanting off to Paris and leave me here high and dry like a frog on a log. You know perfectly well Kate's no use to me socially.'

Cecil couldn't see, any more than any other reasonable man, why she couldn't make do with Kate for a fortnight, but the warm feelings he still cherished for his sister's ex-governess, who would have been Mrs Cecil twenty years ago if Mamma hadn't intervened, moved in his kind heart. It wasn't for Lady Dingle's sake that he was proposing to find someone to take

Miss Bennett's place, if he had to snatch a chimpanzee from the zoo and dress it in a bonnet and skirt; but Kate deserved better from them all than to be left to the vulture's mercy while he and Vi were on their honeymoon.

'Besides, darling,' said Violet, 'you know with your absurd conscience we shouldn't enjoy ourselves a bit. Get her a real battle-axe this time,' she urged. 'Oh, I daresay she'll blunt the edge within six months, but that's better than six weeks, which is about their normal run.'

When Lady Dingle, looking remarkably sprightly and exceedingly well turned out, for all her seventy-four years, got Cecil's telegram announcing that he had engaged a Mrs Appleyard, a widow, and she would be coming down that evening, she said acidly, 'I suppose she finds she can't make two ends meet on her pension. Now that Cecil's engaged to that common little girl he's no thought at all for me.'

'You shouldn't speak of Violet like that,' said Kate Waring, with more warmth than she usually cared to display. 'She's your last hope of grandchildren bearing your name.'

If a table had got up and bitten her Lady Dingle could hardly have been more surprised.

'I consider that a most improper remark from an unmarried woman,' she said. 'Mind you, I could have told Roger he was making a mistake. Dorothy's a devoted wife, I dare say, but a wife's first duty is to give her husband children, and after that first baby that came to nothing . . . I believe she wanted to adopt one, but I had to draw the line there. I shall not leave it a penny in my will, I told Roger, or you either. And he's not done so well in his chosen profession that he can afford to disregard my wishes.' She laughed bitterly. When Roger took silk she had dreamed of seeing his name all over the law reports. 'We must get Roger Dingle,' people would say. And presently, Sir Roger. But he'd just fizzled out, so far as she could see, was never involved in those cases that thrill the public, didn't even touch real crime (like blackmail and murder), which in her opinion was the only road to the kind of publicity she yearned for. When he came to see her she made a point of leaving books lying around—the famous cases of

Marshall-Hall, or Cases in Court by Sir Patrick Hastings. She never said anything beyond, 'Do pass me my book, dear. So fascinating. Why don't you ever tell me any of the details of your trials? It must be a wonderful life.' And to Dorothy, who loved her husband, but had known long ago he was never going to set the Thames on fire, she would observe, 'Men are selfish, aren't they, even the best of them? Roger's always beautifully dressed (which wasn't true) but it never occurs to him to buy you a new fur coat. And it would be a good investment really. Wives are their husband's best trade-mark.'

'Oh, I should like to think I was more than that,' said Dorothy. 'As for a new fur coat, we think we're doing well if we can make both ends meet.'

Lady Dingle sniffed. 'A very poor aspiration! A whiting can do as much.'

Only when Lady Dingle said something about children did Dorothy change; her eyes grew narrow and her manner very quiet.

Roger, finding her one evening in tears in the room that had been his as a boy and had never been redecorated ('scarcely worth it when my children come so seldom to see me,' said Lady Dingle), had implored her, 'Darling, don't let her get under your skin.'

'I shall kill her one of these days, Roger, really I shall. Or worse, I shall say what I think. "I'd sooner die sterile than do to a child of mine what you've done to yours," I shall say. Look at us, kow-towing to her, yes, Roger, you know we do, because she has all the money-bags and we can't save. I'm not blaming you, darling. I don't even care about money, but every time she scoffs at you or brings out one of those beastly success stories I want to shout, "Why didn't you let him have a little capital at the beginning? That's when barristers need help, not twenty-five years later." You had to take anything, go anywhere. She's worse than a murderess, you know she is.'

Roger was horrified. His life wasn't an easy one; like her, he couldn't see other parents with young children without a pang at the heart. Sometimes he wished they'd defied the old woman and adopted a baby, but she had been glorying in ill-health for twenty years and liable to drop off at any time, the doctor said. So why not wait for nature to do her stuff and then start your proxy family with a nice little nest-egg behind you, they'd thought? And here they were twenty years later, too late for even an adopted child now, with Roger past fifty and Dorothy forty-three, and Mamma still looked as if she might be going on for ever.

'Mamma,' said Isobel once, 'will follow the rest of us to the cemetery, wearing crepe and enjoying herself like mad.'

It was perhaps the dispensation of providence that Lady Dingle had no notion of the emotions she aroused in the hearts of those nearest to her.

As soon as she set eyes on Ruth, Lady Dingle said, 'I believe in being frank. It saves time in the long run. Are you in any sort of trouble?'

'I don't know what you mean,' returned Ruth. 'Does one have to be in trouble to take this job?'

'Don't be pert,' snapped Lady Dingle. 'I know practically all there is to be known about companions. I've had them for twenty years. And my impression is that every agency keeps a store of broomsticks and black cats in a side cupboard to issue to the sort of women who apply for this kind of situation. I could furnish a whole Sabbath of witches from my ex-employees alone. You're young and very handsome. You must have been told that. Have you ever been a companion before?'

'I'm a widow,' said Ruth. 'My husband was killed very suddenly in a motoring accident a short time ago. We'd always lived in a good deal of comfort. I hadn't had to work, not even in my own house. Suddenly I found myself without anything, husband, money, home or influence. And I was untrained. It's humiliating to discover how little use you can be.'

'So you think it's humiliating to have to come and work for me?'

'I don't know yet,' said Ruth. 'I meant it was humiliating how few people want to employ you.'

'That's what all my companions have found.' Lady Dingle sounded disappointed. 'They clung to this job like grim death. I suppose they thought the alternative was the workhouse.'

'I shan't stay if I don't like it,' said Ruth.

'Upon my word,' said Lady Dingle, 'I wish that muff of a son of mine hadn't been in such a hurry to get tangled up with that vulgar little girl. You're much more the kind of woman Cecil should have married. Now don't tell me you're going to wear widow's weeds for him all your life, because I shan't believe you. Well, you'd better see your room.' She rang a bell and Kate Waring came in. She was a well-built dark-haired woman in the late forties; she could never have been pretty, but the old-fashioned word comely suited her. She had good features and fine eyes. It seemed odd that she should have stayed at Dingle Hall so long.

'Which room have you given Mrs Appleyard, Kate?'

'The Yellow Room, the one Miss Bennett had.'

'Put her in the Blue room. No, don't argue with me. I'm a good judge of character. Miss Bennett would have slept in the dog-kennel if I'd offered it to her. No spirit, that woman. I hope Mrs Appleyard is going to settle down with us, and in that case she'll be an important member of the household. Now don't frown, Kate. You've lines enough as it is, dashing about in all weathers without a hat. When I was a gel—however, you're not interested, I know. Put Mrs Appleyard in the Blue room—that'll be very convenient for my bedroom in emergencies—and make sure she's got everything. We've had a lot of trouble with companions lately,' she added calmly to Ruth. 'Such a feckless lot, no minds of their own. Like playing ball with someone who never hits it back.'

'She's taken a fancy to you,' said Kate in colourless tones as they went upstairs together. 'I suppose you stood up to her. That's what she wants really. None of the rest of us had the sense, except Isobel. Oh, and Cecil now, but it's twenty years too late for him.'

'Is he being married from the house?' asked Ruth.

'Lady Dingle did suggest it, but Violet said it was normal for a bride to be married from her father's. She's got a father and

stepmother—not on calling terms with Lady Dingle of course.
We're still pretty feudal down here. Lady Dingle would think
it perfectly natural for Violet Ross to curtsy every time they
met.'

Ruth walked across to the window of the Blue room and
looked over the paling evening landscape. The gardens sloped
to a wood and beyond that was the faint blur of water. There
was little colour in the garden and only a few birds flying
home.

'You'll hear the little owl from this room,' said Kate.
'Will it bother you?'

'I grew up in the country,' said Ruth. 'No, I shall appreciate the little owl. Why do you stay here if you feel like that?'
she added, turning back into the room.

'Oh, you get into a rut,' said Kate. 'I came here when I was
eighteen as Isobel's governess. That was in 1925. I had no
degrees; my father died suddenly and I had to get a job. I
wanted to be in the country. Roger was twenty-one and up at
Oxford, Cecil was seventeen, Isobel was ten. It was fun in the
holidays, in spite of Lady Dingle. I was allowed to go riding
and cubbing, oh, at first it was wonderful. I was a country girl
myself, you see. Naturally, I didn't suppose I should be here
nearly thirty years later. But when Isobel went to Paris to finish,
Lady Dingle said I could stay on as housekeeper, I knew the
place. Of course, that's where I went wrong. I should have left
then. I was about the age you are now, and full of what I
meant to do with my life. I never dreamed it would turn out
this way. But each time I thought of leaving it was more difficult than the year before. I'd come to think of this house as my
home. I had no other relatives, my mother was dead, and in
a way I was happy. It was my home,' she repeated. She stopped,
staring. 'I believe Lady Dingle's right, they do send witches
here. I've never talked to anyone like that. You—haven't any
children?'

'I'm like you,' said Ruth equably. 'I haven't anyone. This is
a lovely house.'

'It would be better still if they spent some money on it,'
said Kate. 'If you get into Lady Dingle's good books you might
be able to influence her. Cecil could never do anything, though

41

he's been trying for twenty years. Her answer is that it'll last her time.'

'It's an expensive job,' murmured Ruth.

'Not more than she could manage. That's the trouble, of course. All the money's in her name. Even the business, the shares, are hers. It's all Cecil can do to persuade her to release enough to keep the place watertight.'

A bell rang downstairs and she hurried away. 'What a warning!' reflected Ruth. 'Of course she was in love with Cecil, still is. That's why she stayed. And now I don't suppose she could get another job. Besides, after thirty years they must do something for her.'

She changed into a plain dress of dark peacock-blue and went down to the drawing-room.

'Thank goodness you don't consider a blouse and a dressy skirt the right wear for evening,' ejaculated Lady Dingle. 'That's a nice dress, where did you get it?'

'Paris.' It was the only Paris model Ruth had kept.

'Come down in the world, eh? Ah well, into each life some rain must fall. I used to tell my other companions that. The trouble was they always arrived without their umbrellas.'

Lady Dingle was, more than most people, a creature of impulse; she liked or she disliked, approved or disapproved, according to no accepted code. She had, she said, instincts, and they told her that Ruth Appleyard was an acquisition to the household.

'Thank heaven you have some spirit,' she remarked one day as they sped along the highway in the Vauxhall. 'My last two drove as though they were taking me to the cemetery.'

'You play a remarkably good hand of bridge,' she commented a few days later. 'Who taught you?'

'My husband. We played for money, you see, so we couldn't afford to play anything but well.'

'Tell me about him,' invited Lady Dingle.

'There's nothing much to tell.' Ruth's voice was unemphatic. 'He was thirty-two years old when he died. We'd been married four years. He loved life and was popular, and a lucky gambler, until one day his luck failed.' She told her companion about the crashing of that mighty car.

'Good drivers don't have accidents,' opined Lady Dingle.

'Oh nonsense,' said Ruth, 'you might as well say good doctors never die.'

The situation between Lady Dingle and her new companion was naturally a subject for comment among her children. The old woman made no bones at all about her feelings.

'The first really sensible thing Cecil ever did was to discover Ruth,' she announced. 'And it wouldn't surprise me if it were the last,' she added cruelly, to show that she still disapproved of his marriage.

'Are you a witch?' Isobel asked Ruth curiously on her first visit. 'You certainly seem to have tamed Mamma. Do you find it unbearably dull down here?'

'It doesn't worry me,' said Ruth in her impersonal fashion, 'because it won't go on for ever. Roads are only interminable when you know they'll never come to an end and you can see exactly what they'll be like till the day you die.'

'What a fascinating creature Mrs Appleyard is,' pursued Isobel at a family dinner in Cecil's new house, the following evening. 'Do you suppose she's that romantic thing, an adventuress?'

'I don't see why she stays unless she expects to get something out of it,' said Kate, who was also present. 'And there's no doubt about it, she has your mother at the moment eating out of her hand. I've never seen anything like it in all the years I've been there.'

'I can't imagine how she's done it,' Violet remarked frankly. 'If I handed Lady Dingle so much as a biscuit she'd be sure it was poisoned. Still, it wouldn't surprise me if you were right, about her being an adventuress, I mean. She's certainly glamour with a capital G.' She nodded her small neat head emphatically. 'Do you think she means to cut everybody else out of your mother's will, Isobel?'

'It's difficult not to reflect that Mamma is a very rich woman,' Isobel agreed.

'Cecil doesn't believe that the things that happen in novels ever happen in real life,' Violet continued. 'Perhaps he'll feel differently now. What does she tell you about herself?'

'Nothing,' said Kate, succinctly.

'Whereas the others never stopped telling you their life stories,' broke in Cecil. 'I must say Mamma must find Mrs Appleyard a most refreshing change.'

'Cecil's sold on her, aren't you darling? But then it was you who introduced her into the household. I bet you she's got a thrilling past and sooner or later it'll catch up with her. That'll be the day.'

5

Ruth had come to Dingle Hall in June and now it was approaching the year's end. It was Lady Dingle's practice to allow her companion of the moment four days' holiday at Christmas. This ensured her being out of the way at what the old woman persisted in calling a family festival. Where the companion went was no concern of her employer. Everyone, she said in her sweeping fashion, had relations, and if not relations, some other witch of her own age, she suggested airily. Last year Miss Bennett had come to Kate in tears.

'Lady Dingle tells me I'm not wanted here for Christmas,' she wept. 'Where am I to go?'

'Tell her to join one of those hotel house-parties,' said the dauntless old woman. 'Do her a world of good. Me, too, for really she's like a perpetual fog about the house. I feel my throat rasp and my nose run just to see her.'

As the weeks drew on, until the leaf headed November was torn off the calendar, Kate waited for the old woman to warn Ruth she would be required to make her own Christmas plans, but when she heard nothing of this she took it upon herself to drop the girl a hint.

'A holiday?' exclaimed Ruth. 'Oh no, I don't want a holiday. As a matter of fact, I've nowhere special to go.'

'Nor had Miss Bennett,' was Kate's dry reply.

'You mean, Lady Dingle prefers to have her family to herself? I suppose that's reasonable.'

'I should have thought you knew a lot of people,' murmured Kate, simply.

'You have to know people very well to foist yourself on to them for Christmas. It was different, of course, when my husband was alive.' She thought of Mrs Martin. 'I suppose I could go there.'

'You'd have to give her notice, wouldn't you?'

'Oh, she'd put up a bed on the floor if you turned up without,' Ruth murmured. 'Still, she may have gone north to her brother. Now that Audrey's married so suddenly . . .' She thought of the Devenish household and found, to her surprise, that she would infinitely prefer to stay where she was. However, she hadn't Kate's weakness for looking ahead and apprehending difficulties. And in point of fact she was wise, since Lady Dingle made it perfectly clear to her housekeeper that she had no intention of releasing her companion for the festive week.

'She's a very different proposition from Miss Bennett,' she observed grimly. 'That woman would come to me in tears with a story of an ex-serviceman trying to make enough to give his family a Christmas dinner by selling trash at the back door. When I pointed out that I wasn't interested in trash she'd throw up her hands and say "An EX-SERVICEMAN," as if practically everyone isn't ex-service nowadays and not their own choice as often as not. Ruth deals with them all in the most admirable fashion. I'm not troubled with them at all.'

'No,' thought Kate, 'but we are.' She could never resist that shabby leather attaché case, full of expensive goods she didn't want and that were too costly for her to give to members of the household. The ex-servicemen who visited Lady Dingle never trafficked in anything costing less than a pound; they produced pigskin brushes and steel scissors very finely ground, or bottles of scent . . . Then there was Miss Murfitt from the Mission Church at Bellings Green wanting money for an Old Age Pensioners' Party.

'Let their children ask them home,' said Lady Dingle forcefully. 'That's the trouble nowadays. The State takes over all responsibility and children behave as though their parents had no claims on them whatsoever.'

Kate wrote to Isobel, who didn't come down for Christmas, because the boys had parties locally, but who would bring her husband in the New Year when the children would be staying with school-friends :

'Your mother is arranging for Ruth Appleyard to spend Christmas here. Really, it is an extraordinary situation.

This girl seems to have put a spell on her. Mind you, it makes things much easier for the rest of us. But I can't help wondering if she isn't at her old game of playing one person off against another. If that's so, it will be cruel to Ruth. On the other hand she has the rest of the family on tenterhooks. And only this morning she wrote to Mr Holles asking him to come down. There's only one reason why a woman of your mother's age wants to see her lawyer. Poor Cecil—I met him in the village at lunch-time but he knew nothing of it—he is never sure what she will do next. It doesn't help really that Violet won't play ball, as they say. Logically it should make your mother respect her, but actually I think it has just the opposite result.'

Mr Holles came—a little round paunchy man with a fringe of silver hair and a very correct manner. Lady Dingle saw him alone, and afterwards he remained to lunch. He might have been one of those china figures made to represent the various human virtues—discretion would be his—for all he betrayed of his feelings. Had he been startled? shocked? disapproving? Nobody knew. After lunch he took himself off, having wasted no more words than a miser wastes his pence. As to his reason for coming, Lady Dingle confided in no one.

Now the house was getting down to the final arrangements for the Christmas feast. Tradesmen's carts drove up to the back door, the post was full of Christmas appeals, the postman called with a double knock and a ring at the bell and Kate opened the door; beggars new to the neighbourhood tried their luck and were capably disposed of by Ruth: the only people Lady Dingle consented to see, and this after some demur, were two representatives of the Gentlewomen's Self-Help Society, who called with samples of hand-made embroidery and baby clothes.

'Which are you suggesting I shall buy?' Lady Dingle enquired, when Ruth reported their arrival.

'I've looked at some of the babies' things,' said Ruth, diplomatically. 'They're very simple and well-made and a good deal cheaper than the stuff in the shops of the same quality.'

'How many have come? Half the Society?'

'Two,' Ruth smiled. 'They always go in pairs, I believe.'

'I wonder why,' said Lady Dingle grimly. 'Don't trust each other, I suppose. All right, you can send them up, but don't hold out any hopes. It's just that I shall have to buy Violet's baby something and this would be as good as anything else.'

The elderly women came in carrying a large hold-all. They spread their goods all over the table.

'I'm not setting up a shop,' said Lady Dingle, irritably.

'We should like to show you everything,' said the visitors in untroubled tones.

'I simply want to look at two or three matinée jackets or vests or whatever it is children wear nowadays.'

The women went on unpacking their goods.

'Don't let us detain you, Ruth,' murmured Lady Dingle, sarcastically. 'I expect you've plenty to do.'

Ruth went in search of Kate, whom she found in the morning room trimming the Christmas tree.

'How surprising!' said Ruth. 'Seeing there are no children coming I wouldn't have expected Lady Dingle to have a tree.'

'There's always been a tree,' returned Kate, biting her lip in anger at this interruption. The tree was her special glory and delight. It carried her back to the years when she was young and still believed in hope. 'Hope,' she thought, 'it's like a bird. You think at last you've tamed it and you open the door, but instead of hopping on to your finger it flies madly away, shrieking derisively from the curtain-rod or some perch where you can't reach it.' ('Really, Kate,' Lady Dingle would have said, 'have you taken leave of your senses? Hope a bird indeed! What nonsense! You're as bad as Miss Bliss.' Miss Bliss had read poetry aloud in her room in the evening and had brought half the household up at midnight dramatising 'The Ancient Mariner.' Kate read poetry too but refrained from public recitals.) None of the other companions had ever offered to help with the tree and Kate guarded her privilege jealously.

'What enchanting decorations!' exclaimed Ruth, taking one up. 'Where did you find them?'

'They're the ones we used when Isobel was in the schoolroom. I never let anyone else handle them, and I always put them away myself when the week's over. Did you never have a tree?' she added curiously.

Ruth shook her head. 'Jack and I were hardly ever at home for Christmas. And when we were he said holly marked the walls and made trouble with the landlord and the tree does shed its needles everywhere. I did suggest mistletoe, but he said that any party that needed mistletoe wouldn't use it, if you get me.'

Kate wasn't sure she did, but all she said was, 'But before that—when you were a child?'

Ruth shook her head. 'No. Aunt Theo—' and then she stopped.

'Who was Aunt Theo?'

'She looked after the house for us. I lost my mother when I was very young.'

'Did you never have a proper Christmas?'

Ruth smiled and picked up a glittering peacock with a spun glass tail.

'That depends what you mean by a proper Christmas.' She balanced the bird on the tree. 'What happens here? Do they go to church—or what?'

'Lady Dingle listens to the service on the wireless with a running commentary. Roger and Dorothy consider themselves civilised, so they don't go to church at all. Cecil and Violet, of course, won't appear till lunchtime. It wouldn't surprise me a bit to know Violet goes to church, in which case I don't doubt Cecil will go with her. What about you?'

Ruth shook her head. 'Oh, I'm civilised, too.'

'As for this cousin or whatever it is Dorothy's bringing down he can do as he likes.'

'Who's he?' asked Ruth idly, straightening the fairy queen's wand.

'He's called Frank Hardy and Dorothy says he's young. That could be anything up to forty. You don't have to help me if you don't want to,' she added, rather desperately.

'But I love it,' said Ruth, absorbed. 'I've always wanted to deck a tree.'

'Didn't your friend—Mrs Martin—have one?'

'I expect so, but I was never there for Christmas. I only stayed a few months, after I came south, and before I married.'

In spite of having said she wanted to help she seemed to tire suddenly, hung a glittering silver ball, fixed a toy cat at the junction of a branch and then, with a murmur, went away.

Having stormed a citadel hitherto regarded as impregnable, the two representatives of the Gentlewomen's Self-Help were determined to have a field day.

'I'm not expecting my daughter-in-law to produce triplets,' protested Lady Dingle, but for once she had met her match. Every available piece of furniture was utilised as a display stand.

'She'll never let them in again,' Ruth murmured to Kate. 'Do you think we dare interrupt?'

'I thought they might have something I could buy for Christmas,' said Kate. 'I detest shopping, and you said their prices were moderate.'

But when they braved Lady Dingle's sitting-room they found her alone, with a little pile of garments beside her.

'Oh, I got rid of them some time ago,' she assured them. 'They were perfectly prepared to camp here from now till Christmas. Some people appear to think the rest of the world is as unoccupied as themselves.'

Kate picked up one of the little matinée jackets. 'I should think Violet will be delighted with these,' she observed, diplomatically.

'I doubt it.' Lady Dingle sounded sceptical. 'It wouldn't surprise me if she let the baby roam about stark naked, like the pagan she is. Take care, Kate, where you put that down. There's a blob of ink—get some blotting-paper.'

Ruth found it, then in her turn praised the fine workmanship. 'When we were abroad,' she said, and almost for the first time she used the plural unconsciously, 'we used to see the loveliest work done by the nuns, underclothes with exquisite embroidery —it seemed so strange.'

'I suppose you'd have liked them to concentrate on shrouds as being more seemly, but who's going to buy them? Oh, they've got their heads screwed on all right, old Dilly and Dally. It wouldn't surprise me to know those are their real names. The older one—Dilly—tried to tell me they hadn't any change. Thought I'd buy something else, of course, to make up the amount. But I'm not so easily fooled. In that case, I said, you'd better take back that little jacket . . . They found the change all right then.'

The rain came on suddenly after lunch, so Lady Dingle didn't go out, as she'd intended. Instead she busied herself with the remainder of her Christmas letters (*Too late for Christmas? Then they'll get a nice surprise in the New Year*). Surrounded by ink, paper, envelopes, sealing-wax, matches and the letters she was proposing to answer, she spent a busy afternoon, and left a pile of correspondence on the hall-table to be given to the postman when he called next day.

Violet, who was expecting her baby in late April, opened her mother-in-law's letter regarding Christmas arrangements, glanced through it and tossed it across the table to her husband.

'Royal Command,' she said. 'O.K. for you, darling?'

Cecil looked surprised. 'We've always been with Mother at Christmas.'

'You've never had a wife before. I've got a home, too. Still, for you, darling, no sacrifice is too great, and, to be candid, with four adults and five children at home and only one bathroom I do think you'd be better off at Dingle Hall. Wouldn't it be lovely if it was a white Christmas?'

But the snow held off. There was only frost that made Roger, driving his wife and her new-found Canadian cousin, Frank Hardy, down to Dingle Hall, proceed with more than his normal caution.

'You're very quiet, Frank,' Dorothy teased him.

Frank smiled absently, but said nothing.

'I wonder what this Mrs Appleyard is really like,' Dorothy went on. 'She's been with Lady D. for six months now, and we haven't heard a single complaint about her. Have we, Roger? I call it ominous.'

'Oh come, my dear,' remonstrated her husband, 'you're letting your imagination fly away with you. I know Christmas is the season for fairy-tales, but you should keep within bounds. My wife,' he added, turning politely to Frank, 'is convinced that Mrs Appleyard is a woman with a past, who's going to inveigle my mother into leaving her all her fortune, and then, presumably, see to it that she inherits without delay. You should be writing thrillers, Dorothy. That kind of thing doesn't happen in real life.'

Still Frank said nothing; it seemed to him quite possible that it might. But, even so, he hadn't a notion what the next few weeks were to hold or how they would revolutionise his entire existence.

6

Kate opened the door to the travellers; the only servants were two daily women called Mrs Gusset and Mrs Gamp, who were never seen in the front part of the house. She greeted Roger and Dorothy, shook hands with Frank and took them into the drawing-room. Lady Dingle said composedly, 'It's very nice of you to come and cheer us up. Ruth!'

The woman standing in the window turned. A shaft of afternoon sunlight struck the young man, gilding his fair head and handsome brown face. For an instant fate played tricks with her; once again she saw Jack Appleyard coming towards her. She had recovered herself an instant later, but that moment of dismay and shock hadn't escaped the young man. He put out his hand.

'Mrs Appleyard!'

'How do you do?' What an actress the woman was. You'd never guess they'd met before and in what circumstances. It didn't occur to him that she might genuinely not recognise him, having on that earlier occasion no room in her eye for any face but her husband's. Kate brought in the tea and poured it out. They settled down and conversation became general. Dorothy noted with dismay, that whereas no other companion had been treated like a member of the family, Ruth took her place in the circle with the utmost aplomb. It was a relief when Cecil and Violet arrived a little later. Violet's condition was by now perfectly obvious and she did nothing to conceal it. 'Why should I?' she said. 'There's nothing indecent about having a baby. We all made our mothers equally conspicuous once upon a time,' though in private she added to her husband, 'I have a secret doubt about your mother ever really giving birth at all. I believe she did find you in a water-lily or under a gooseberry bush or something. Dorothy's cousin is a poppet,' she added.

'Did you see the way he was watching Ruth? He won't be popular with my dear mother-in-law if he starts giving her ideas.'

'After about five minutes' acquaintance? Sometimes, Vi, you talk quite amazing nonsense. This isn't one of your penny novelettes remember.'

'Not a penny novelette perhaps,' Violet allowed, 'if there are any such things these days. But the situation has practically all the conditions demanded by a thriller. Old house, rich old dowager, pinched heirs, faithful housekeeper, mysterious female companion. All that's been lacking to date has been a hero—and here's Frank Hardy simply made to measure. Why, it's quite, quite perfect.'

Before Cecil could reply Frank Hardy came across to them saying, 'Excuse me! I think Lady Dingle is trying to attract our attention.'

The old woman was, indeed, about to make an announcement. 'Christmas is supposed to be a time of relaxation,' she said, 'certainly not a time for business discussions. But it is so seldom that I have all my family under my roof simultaneously that I can't neglect this opportunity. And I suggest that we should get rid of this detail before the festivities start. It's purely a family matter . . .' She paused, and Kate said cheerfully, 'Mr Hardy, let me show you your room. I expect you'll be wanting to unpack.'

'And afterwards,' said Ruth, neatly picking up her cue, 'perhaps I could give you a hand, Kate.'

'All hands to the wheel,' crowed the old woman with a derisive grin. 'You can tell it's Christmas, can't you, when everyone's so anxious to be helpful.'

As the door closed behind them, the departing trio heard the old woman's voice. 'As I think you know, Mr Holles has recently paid me a visit.' Then the door closed and they heard no more.

'I hope you won't lose your way in this house,' said Kate in friendly tones, conducting the young man up the main stairway. 'We've had to put you at the farther end of the corridor . . .'

'I do hope Lady Dingle doesn't mind me butting in,' said

Frank. 'Dorothy assured me it would be all right.'

'Do you play bridge?' asked Kate.

'Well.' He sounded cautious. 'I can count the pips.'

'In that case you'll be well advised to say you don't. They take it very seriously here.'

'You play?' he murmured.

Kate shook her head. 'Years ago I went to lunch with a friend in London who'd just joined a woman's club. She was very proud of it and wanted to show me round. We opened a door —I think she wasn't quite certain herself which room it was— and it proved to be the bridge room. There were four tables occupied and, as we looked in, sixteen pairs of eyes glared at us over fans of cards. I felt exactly as if I'd got into the wolf enclosure at the zoo. I've never touched a card since, except for an occasional game of rummy.'

'I'm an expert at washing up,' Frank offered, helpfully.

'Then you'll be a very popular guest. Here you are.' She opened the door of a typical 'bachelor's room', which meant it was small and a long way from the nearest bathroom and had a rug instead of a carpet on the floor. Not that that bothered him, he wasn't used to luxury in the Fulham Road. 'If anything's been forgotten you must let me know,' said Kate.

All the doubts he had experienced in the court in Italy rushed over him again. Once more he saw Ruth, beautiful and troubled, standing by the lordly white car. And again his doubts clouded his mind. He wondered if they'd ever know the truth about that afternoon. Better not, perhaps, seeing the shape it would most probably assume. What did she hope to achieve here, he asked himself? The answer to that was not hard to find. The household might be dull, the duties monotonous, but it was impossible to forget that Lady Dingle was a very wealthy old woman, in indifferent health (according to Dorothy) for all her surface vigour, an unpredictable old tyrant (that was Dorothy, too). He didn't like it one bit. And he couldn't put out of his mind Crook's story about young Ruth Garside. He felt pretty certain that no one at Dingle Hall had an inkling of that story. Should he, perhaps, drop a hint— to Roger, say? He owed it really to him, as his host. And yet —and yet—why stick your neck out? Crook had inquired.

'Keep your mouth shut, it's only for three days. And though you may be your brother's keeper there's nothing in the Good Book about a cousin about fourteen times removed.'

And, of course, he reminded himself, he had no proof that Ruth Appleyard would be a penny better off if her employer died tonight.

He finished his unpacking, which didn't take long, and went to stand by the window. A figure was going down the shadowy path, a cloak concealing the shape, but he had no doubt whose it was. On an impulse he caught up his own coat and ran downstairs to overtake her.

'I hope you won't lose your way,' Kate had said, and he had laughed. He was accustomed to finding his way in strange countries and the idea that he could lose himself within the confines of a house was absurd. Nevertheless, that was precisely what happened. He remembered they'd come along a passage and turned a corner, but he had been talking so eagerly, and was at the same time so much concerned with the situation in which he found himself, that he hadn't memorised the precise direction they had taken. So, when he reached the foot of the stairs, he found he wasn't in the hall, as he'd anticipated, but in a narrow passage leading, obviously, to the kitchen quarters. On one side of him was a door an inch or so ajar and covered from the farther side by a heavy velvet portière. While he was still considering which way to go next voices came to his ear.

'My dear Mother!' It was Roger speaking. 'I really think you've taken leave of your senses. You can't mean you're going to leave this immense sum to a girl you've only known for six months and cut Kate's legacy to a miserable five hundred pounds, after thirty years' service with us.'

'It's nice to know you're so prosperous that you can regard five hundred pounds as a miserable sum,' retorted Lady Dingle, spiritedly. 'And you mustn't forget that Kate has enjoyed a very comfortable family life practically as one of ourselves for a generation. That should be taken into account. And finally,' she added, her voice rising as someone, presumably Roger, tried to interrupt, 'you must remember that Ruth Appleyard is in a rather different category from your sister's ex-governess. *She* is a very attractive and gifted young woman, who could get something more amusing tomorrow than dancing attendance on an old woman. People like that can command a premium, as you, my dear Cecil, realised when you agreed, on my behalf and without consulting me, to pay her practically three times as much as any other companion I have ever had.'

'She may be everything you say,' said Roger, 'but I don't think even Mrs Appleyard would find it easy to get another employer prepared to leave her ten thousand pounds in her will.'

'I see you agree with me,' murmured Lady Dingle in a deceptively cosy voice. 'Kate, of course, is a woman of good sense who appreciates which side her bread is buttered. She knows that women of fifty with no particular qualifications are a drug on the market. I should know. I've had plenty of them here; she can't drive a car or play a decent hand of bridge. Oh, I'm not afraid of Kate flinging up her heels and going off. If she'd meant to do that she'd have taken her opportunity a quarter of a century ago. But Mrs Appleyard needs to be bribed (since that's the word in all your minds, I can see) to spend some of her best years at Dingle Hall. And don't forget,' she wound up. 'she only gets the money if she's with me at the time of my death, and on the whole I think I take a more optimistic view of my chances of survival than either of my sons.'

'It's not fair to the girl,' exploded Roger. 'Suppose there were some accident—even the best drivers are sometimes involved through no fault of their own—and it came out, as it must, that you'd left her this preposterous sum, gossip would create a most unpleasant situation for her.'

'There aren't many situations that can't be cured by a legacy of that size,' retorted his mother, composedly. 'I daresay Ruth would survive a little malice. Or are you suggesting she'd engineer a motor smash, contriving to be unhurt herself? Well, I recognised from the outset that she was an ambitious gel, but I never thought she might go so far as that. I like spirit myself . . . Violet, my dear, we haven't heard you say anything?'

'Because it's all poppycock,' said Violet scornfully. 'I don't believe people go round committing murder just for money. If she was being blackmailed, or if you had some hold over someone she was in love with, but money . . .'

'I have yet to learn that people are so—oblivious—to money as that. I'm afraid you're an idealist, Violet. Cecil now . . .'

'Daddy would give Cecil a manager's job in his works any time,' said Violet carelessly. 'He's offered it him already, and I wish he'd take it. But Cecil's got such a conscience—I always told myself I wouldn't marry a conscientious man. It's worse to live with than—' she stopped herself just in time.

'Than a mother-in-law? My dear Violet, that's the first time I've ever found you—inhibited, isn't that the word you young people use nowadays?—since our first meeting.' She didn't actually say 'regrettable meeting' but the implication would have been obvious to a blind man. 'Really, Cecil, this is very interesting. I'm not at all sure I shouldn't advise you to accept.'

'Oh, Vi wasn't serious,' exclaimed Cecil sounding as apprehensive as doubtless he looked. 'Naturally I shouldn't give up the estate. It's been in the family for generations.'

His mother chuckled. 'So have I been in the family for generations but even I can't last for ever. And as people—and things—get older they become correspondingly more expensive. I must admit there seems very little return for the expenditure, and I have no wish to hold out hopes that may not be fulfilled.'

'What precisely does that mean?'

'I'm sure Violet understands,' chortled the old woman.

'Your mother means she won't guarantee to leave you enough out of your father's fortune to keep things running. Everyone knows you can't keep estate work going without some capital for bad weather, and of course there's never been any chance to accumulate it. If there'd been a pocket of capital, as there should have been . . .'

'My dear Violet, you are a little presumptuous, are you not? It's one thing to dictate to the living, though perhaps neither courteous nor particularly discreet, but when you attempt to dictate to the dead . . .'

'I'd dictate to Old Nick himself if I thought it would do Cecil any good,' said Violet fiercely.

At this stage Frank heard a door open somewhere near at hand and came to his senses with a start. He had been so much engrossed in what he had overheard he had scarcely realised he was eavesdropping. He moved forward and round the bend of the passage. Opposite him was the kitchen door and Kate was coming towards him.

'Pride goes before a fall,' he murmured ruefully. 'I did lose my way.'

'You took the wrong staircase,' said Kate. 'Where were you trying to get to?'

'I was going to walk round the garden. I'm not afraid of a little fresh air and I'm used to a Canadian winter when it really is cold. Seeing there's a family conclave in process,' he added quickly, 'I thought it might be more tactful to be out of the way for a little while.'

'You can get out along here,' said Kate, leading the way. 'Though I doubt if the conclave goes on much longer. If it does, I shall risk having my head bitten off and break it up. Lady Dingle isn't as strong as she looks and there's something about relations that seems to bring out the worst in everyone. Besides, I don't think Violet should be allowed to get worked up and she and Lady Dingle react unfavourably at sight.'

'What a nice girl she is,' murmured Frank.

Kate turned to him. 'Take another word of advice, Mr Hardy. Tell Cecil that, if you like, but not Lady Dingle. She's of the line of the great dictators, you know, and this marriage wasn't one of her plans. Since you're spending a few days with us it's as well to be frank. These occasions are a nightmare to me. I never know when someone won't blow a fuse.'

Frank smiled sympathetically and went into the grounds. He wondered if Kate knew about the most recent will that, so far as he could gather from what he had overheard, virtually disinherited her. He imagined that the brothers would see to it she didn't starve, but it's one thing to have a legacy by right and another to be compelled to accept an allowance; and he thought Kate was the independent type who'd feel she ought to go on working. He wondered, too, how much Ruth Appleyard knew about this latest will.

7

Ruth's start of surprise and shock at the sight of Frank Hardy had nothing to do with that momentary meeting on the Riviera coast, for, in truth, she had not recognised him. But he had been so poignant a reminder of the husband she had loved for four years and lost in a moment of self-betrayal that she felt she couldn't stand the confines of four walls. She realised now that ever since his death she had been existing rather than living; she had demanded little except the absence of active suffering, and so had sought an environment as different as possible from any she had known during her days as Jack Appleyard's wife. Now Frank Hardy, simply by walking through the door, had changed all that. He had, as it were, pushed aside the stone and revealed the skeleton concealed in the sepulchre. Sooner or later, she now knew, she must return to the business of active living. 'I'm no more than an invalid here,' she reminded herself.

The ghosts of other Christmases rose up before her, seasons of gaiety and amusement, of lights, colour and, above all, of youth. Being at Dingle Hall was like spending your time in the wings of the theatre while the play went on just out of sight. She remembered her last Christmas with Jack; they'd spent it in London, a gaily-lit capital full of their friends, there had been dancing, suppers after the play, lovely clothes and a new ring—well that had gone to settle the accounts in Bordighera, but how she'd loved it (and its giver) at the time. She contrasted that occasion with the present, a houseful of middle-aged people, Roger and Dorothy, Cecil and Kate . . . The sudden arrival of a contemporary had wakened her abruptly from a kind of drugged sleep.

Her thoughts had carried her, unnoticing, through the garden and the blue wooden gate in the wall that separated the orchard from the wilder land beyond. Here was the ornamental water with its rustic bridge and carefully preserved island in the centre where a pair of swans nested every year. Lady Dingle was proud of her swans, prouder, Ruth sometimes thought, than she was of her two sons.

Here everything was so quiet the atmosphere had a magical quality. It was hard to remember that houseful of suspicious and warring people not five minutes away. The shadows had deepened and now the lake was merely a dim oval on which shadows moved, as the ducks swam in the little pool they had made in the thin ice. A long plaintive cry assailed her ears and, glancing upwards, she could just distinguish the pair of swans flying overhead, their wings outstretched, seeming to float on the iron-grey air. The cry died away and the silence came back. She was as remote from the world as the prisoner in Poe's terrible story of *The Pit and the Pendulum*.

She shivered, suddenly aware of the coldness of the wind, the icy impersonality of the over-arching sky. A step sounded behind her and she turned, suppressing an exclamation of alarm.

'Don't be nervous,' said Frank Hardy, stepping through a small clump of trees to stand at her side. 'I'm not a ghost, and perhaps you half wish I were. I wanted to have a word with you, Mrs. Appleyard, and with the family engaged in a deadly clinch this seemed a good opportunity.'

'I can't imagine why you should want to talk to me,' said Ruth bluntly.

'You've put me in a very awkward situation,' the young man pointed out. 'Do you believe in a pattern in life?'

'If it exists, it's quite incomprehensible.'

'That's what Crook says. Still, I wonder. The saints used to say we couldn't understand it because we only saw it from the wrong side. You haven't forgotten our meeting in Ventimiglia, have you?'

'In . . .? Oh!' The change in her voice seemed so genuine that for an instant he really believed her greeting of him as a stranger wasn't an act, after all. 'Was it you, that day?'

'Yes. You didn't notice me at the inquest on your husband?'

'No. Were you there? Why, particularly? I mean, you didn't know Jack, did you?'

'I suppose you could call it curiosity. I wanted to know how it happened that a man who was an ace driver, as apparently he was, could take a car out on a stiff hill when he knew it wasn't running perfectly. Well, you explained that at the inquest. He didn't know, because he hadn't been warned.'

'Since you were at the inquest you'll realise why,' said Ruth steadily. 'Did you follow me here to talk about my husband, Mr Hardy?'

He said again in a meditative voice, 'You've put me in a tight corner, Mrs Appleyard. Will you tell me something?'

'I don't know till you ask.'

'Does Lady Dingle know about Ruth Garside?'

The blow was so unexpected, so nearly mortal, that this time a sound not loud enough to be a cry, more like a protracted moan, escaped her.

'What's Ruth Garside to you?'

'I asked you just now if you believed in a pattern in life. Back in London in the fall I met a man who knew of the link between Ruth Garside and Ruth Appleyard. And then I come down here, the first country house, if that's what you call it, I've stayed in since I landed in Europe, and here you are again. It's almost too much to be sheer coincidence.'

'Perhaps I'm dense,' said Ruth. 'I still don't see the point of this conversation. Or—had you blackmail in mind? An old lady's companion isn't a very fruitful subject for blackmail. And, if you stayed long enough in Ventimiglia to make full enquiries, I'm sure some kind soul told you that after my husband's death I had to sell practically everything I had to raise my fare home.'

'I hadn't thought of blackmail, certainly not in the meaning in which you use the word. But—does Lady Dingle know about the affair at Nether Milton?'

'Not from me. It's hardly the kind of thing one would want to boast about.'

'And do either of her sons . . .?'

'I shouldn't think so.'

'Then, can't you see what an invidious position you're in?

Suppose something happened to Lady Dingle, some accident, say, all that past history would be raked up.'

'Why should it? You speak as if her death would be an advantage to me. I should simply have lost a job.'

'Oh Ruth,' he said, softly, 'as if you didn't know.'

'Know what?' Her voice was as sharp as the night wind.

'Why do you stay?' he countered.

'It's odd you should ask that. Just before you came up I was thinking it was almost time for me to make a move.'

'Ah!' There was no mistaking the relief in his voice. 'If that's true that resolves my difficulties. When were you thinking of going?'

'When it suits me. This is the most extraordinary conversation I ever had. I can't see what on earth it is to do with you.'

'No? Use a little imagination. Put yourself in my place. Suppose I'd had a wife who had died rather mysteriously because I hadn't warned her the car wasn't running true; suppose, moreover, that some years ago I'd been tried for attempted murder; suppose you came to a house by chance, or even by providential design, and found me the confidant of a rich old woman, who was prepared to make me independent if I stayed with her for the rest of her life.'

She interrupted. 'I don't think my imagination would take me that far.'

'It wouldn't have to,' said Frank. 'You mustn't think me more of a fool than, in fact, I am. You've been offered a very powerful inducement to stay, haven't you?'

'I don't know what you're talking about,' said Ruth, and now apprehension gave way to impatience. 'I thought you only met Lady Dingle for the first time today.'

'You knew the lawyer had been down, though, so you must have guessed she had changes in mind.'

'She hasn't confided in me,' said Ruth.

'No? Well, I still think you'd be wise to pack your traps and look for another job. But that's what you're going to do, isn't it? You've just said so.'

'What you've just told me, though how you know is beyond me, puts rather a different complexion on things, doesn't it?

I'm sick of this skirmishing, Mr Hardy.'

'Frank,' he interrupted. 'After all, we're not precisely strangers. All right. I happen to know that Lady Dingle means to leave you something handsome in her will.'

'And you grudge it me?'

He said, 'Look, I'll make you an offer. Tell Lady Dingle the facts about yourself. You're well dug in here, she likes you, she trusts you, this would be as good a time as any . . . What's that, Ruth Appleyard? You won't?'

Ruth had a vision of the tough old woman faced with the truth. She hadn't the smallest doubt of the result of her candour.

'Well, my dear,' she'd say, 'you're a fine driver and a good bridge player and it's nice for me to see a young face around the house. But all the same, I'd just as soon not have my tea brought me by someone who was once accused of trying to poison an old man; and, come to that, I'm not sure I'm so keen about being driven by a woman whose husband met his death in a car accident in circumstances that have never been satisfactorily explained. I believe it's a fact that drivers often survive accidents when passengers don't. So here's a present and it's been nice knowing you, but this is like that old Victorian melodrama—the parting of the ways.'

Yes, reflected Ruth, that's how it would be. She'd be mad to tell.

'You tell me something now,' she suggested, after a pause during which she was shaken with such anger as seemed to swing her back to little Ruth Garside flinging a knife at her father in the kitchen of Nether Milton. 'Do you intend to follow me round wherever I go in the hope that sooner or later I'll throw up the sponge and put myself into the river?'

'There are jobs unconnected with rich cantankerous old women who enjoy thwarting their families,' Frank reminded her. 'Think it over, Ruth, and remember, if anything should happen, you've already got the whole family up in arms. No, I don't say it's your fault, but there's no sense in not facing facts.'

'I wonder why you should suppose this is any concern of yours?'

'Oh, didn't I explain? I believe in a pattern. And for another thing, I don't fancy the idea of you in another court case, even if it's only in the witness-box. Maybe you've had gambler's luck to date, but even Gambler's Luck crosses his feet sooner or later.'

As they walked back to the house she said in more controlled tones, 'It would make you look a bit silly, wouldn't it, if Lady Dingle did have a sudden heart attack or something and it was learned that she'd only left me a bit of jewellery?'

'I should probably pass out from absolute shock,' he assured her. 'But, as I said earlier, you mustn't suppose I'm such a fool I speak without the book. I imagine the conclave will be over by now. I must get ready to sing for my supper.'

In the house the atmosphere was as brittle as the icing on a Christmas cake. The argument was over, but it had left its marks on them all. Lady Dingle was at her most arrogant; a doctor might have diagnosed incipient hysteria. When dinner was over she insisted they should play bridge.

'Roger will play, of course. And Cecil. Violet, you don't play, I know. How about you, Mr Hardy?'

'I'm better at snap,' acknowledged Frank.

'Then, Ruth, you can make a four. Dorothy will probably like to chat to Violet.'

'I ought to be going home,' said Violet calmly. 'These late hours aren't good for the son and heir, and I don't want any child of mine to be a Nightlife Nicky. It's all right, Cec. I can drive myself home.'

'Of course you won't. Mother, can't you make up a four without me?'

'How?' asked Lady Dingle in her most disagreeable voice. 'Mr Hardy only plays snap, which is about Dorothy's level. Kate doesn't play at all, even if she hadn't other work to occupy her.' She looked as if she were about to explode with apoplexy. Her eyes burned like stars in frost and were equally hard; under them the skin was dark and bruised; an ugly flush had come up in her cheeks, her hands trembled.

'All right,' agreed Cecil. 'I'll drive Vi home and then come back. It shouldn't take more than about a quarter of an hour.'

He was as good as his word, but the intervening fifteen

minutes didn't do Lady Dingle's temper any good. She sat lightly drumming her fingers on the surface of the table, and answering all attempts at conversation in monosyllables. When Cecil returned they cut for partners and Roger sighed almost audibly when he saw he was to play with his mother. Nor were his fears misplaced.

Before long, Frank, talking to Dorothy in a window embrasure, heard the old woman say, 'It's nice, Roger, to know you can afford to throw money away so lightly. I should have thought it would have been obvious to a child where the last trump lay.'

'Mrs Appleyard's too good for me,' said Roger with an attempt at a laugh. 'The fact is I don't get as much practice as I'd like . . .'

'Ha! Ha!' said the old woman. 'First time I've ever known you make a pun. If you don't pay more attention to your briefs than you do to your cards, it doesn't surprise me you stuck a quarter of the way up the ladder.'

Frank felt the woman next to him shaking with rage and despair. His hand closed over her. 'Shall I create a diversion?' he offered. 'See a stranger lurking in the grounds? or smash a window?'

'One of these days,' whispered Dorothy, 'I shall murder the old brute. I wish Roger had listened to me and we'd spent Christmas at home. It's going to be horrid for you, too. But he said he couldn't afford to offend her. She holds the purse-strings, that was an infamous will her husband made, but of course he was putty in her hands . . .' Her voice was low but furious; he let her ramble on, he thought most likely she didn't know what she was saying. Her eyes were fixed on her husband's ashy face. It was a relief to them all when Kate came in with a hot drink for Lady Dingle and an intimation that the whisky and syphon were set out in the library.

'Perhaps we should give Roger his whisky before the cards next time,' suggested Roger's mother maliciously. But her bad temper had passed. For the second rubber she had cut with Ruth, and they had swept the decks. Like many rich people, nothing delighted Lady Dingle more than to make thirty or forty shillings by her wits.

'One of these days, Ruth,' she remarked pleasantly when the three men had gone off to the library, 'you should set up a bridge club. Preferably in London. You'd be a delightful hostess.'

Ruth smiled. 'Jack and I used to think of that, but we never seemed to have the right amount of capital at the right time.'

The old woman rubbed her hands. 'Everything comes to him who waits. Is patience one of the seven deadly virtues? I never can remember. If it isn't, it should be.'

Ruth smiled. 'You don't really believe that?'

Lady Dingle laughed and put an affectionate hand on the girl's arm. 'Perhaps I agree with you, that sometimes it's even better to go out and take what you want. It's what I've always done.' She chuckled meaningly. Dorothy looked away; she felt sick. What more evidence did they require that tonight's revelations hadn't been an example of the old woman's misplaced humour, just for the pleasure of making them squirm, with no actual intention behind it? No, she was absolutely in earnest. Roger was her son, Cecil had been her slave for twenty years, Kate had a lifetime of service in the family, but she both threatened and intended to throw them all over for the sake of this smart, smooth-spoken adventuress. 'She shall not,' Dorothy promised herself, fiercely. 'I'd sooner strangle her myself. After all these years of humiliation and silence, Roger shall *not* be cheated of his rights.'

Lady Dingle looked across the room. 'Aren't you feeling well, Dorothy? You look like an avenging fury. Come, Ruth, I'm going up to bed. You might read to me a little when I'm tucked up. Mrs Appleyard has a voice like a snake-charmer's pipe,' she added, in a voice brittle with malice, yet gay, almost raffish. 'The cobra simply lowers her head and goes—right—off—to—sleep.'

'Roger,' said his wife in the rather bleak main spare room about an hour later, 'is there nothing you can do about that will? I thought at first it might be a joke in rather bad taste, but she's deathly serious. And Mrs Appleyard will stay here and collect, as they say.'

'She'd be a great fool if she didn't,' said Roger simply. 'If you're going to suggest that my mother's *non compos mentis*

I should put the idea out of your mind. There wouldn't be a chance of proving anything of the sort. And in any case we should have Holles dead against us, and he carries quite a lot of professional ballast. Still,' he added more comfortingly, 'you know how changeable mother is; she makes a new will about every eighteen months. Mrs Appleyard may have worn out her welcome by then.'

'Alternatively, perhaps she'll come into the money before your mother has time to make another will. She looked really old tonight for the first time, Roger, like one of those puppets you make with sticks and string that can seem so animated, but under the satin gown . . .'

Roger said sharply, 'We're none of us at our best tonight, I think. Kate seemed rather on edge, too. Do you suppose Mamma has told her how she's affected by the new will?'

'It's not the money that's upset Kate,' returned Dorothy, shrewdly. 'It's seeing Violet carrying Cecil's child. You know, I believe she'd have done better to ride the storm twenty years ago and marry Cecil in the teeth of Mamma's disapproval. Suppose she had disowned him? He could have got another job. But Kate was afraid he'd turn against her because she'd cost him so much . . .'

'My dear Dorothy, all this mulling over the past is horribly morbid and probably your conclusions are incorrect. Kate's always been charming to Violet. The fact is, everyone gets overwrought at these Christmas gatherings. I wouldn't have come this year if I hadn't particularly wanted to get in the old lady's good books. Thank goodness, she seems to have taken to Frank Hardy. And now let's get some sleep. We shall have plenty of strain on our nerves tomorrow.'

Tomorrow's only an hour away,' murmured Dorothy. She yawned. 'I get more tired in this house than anywhere else in the world. I should like to sleep right through till lunch-time but I suppose if I asked for breakfast in bed your mother would take it as an insult. I hope I don't live to be old. I hope . . .'

Roger put out his hand and switched off the light. He was pretty near breaking-point himself, nearer than she knew.

8

The commotion broke out in the small hours of Christmas Day. It was not quite four o'clock when Dorothy woke from a heavy and uneasy sleep to the sounds of activity going on all about her. Doors opened and closed, feet sounded in the passage. She groaned. 'It can't be morning yet.' She put on the bedside lamp and glanced at her watch. Outside her door a voice said clearly, 'I'll ring him up. He won't be pleased, but . . .'

In an instant she seemed wide-awake, was out of bed and pulling on her dressing-gown. Catching her husband by the shoulder she implored, 'Wake up, something's going on,' and, without waiting for his response, opened the door. Kate in her familiar red woollen dressing-gown stood at the head of the stairs. Ruth, in a smartly-cut dark blue garment that even Dorothy recognised as an American 'lounging robe', was like a sentinel in front of Lady Dingle's door.

'What's going on?' demanded Dorothy in a rather high voice.

Both women turned. 'Ruth doesn't like the look of Lady Dingle,' said Kate. 'She's unconscious and it's not a natural sleep. She thinks it may be a stroke. I'm going to get Dr Freeman.'

'At four o'clock in the morning? But why—I don't mean Dr Freeman, I mean why did anyone go into her room at four o'clock? If she was unconscious, she couldn't have cried out.'

'I generally go in once during the night,' Ruth explained. 'That's why my room is so close to hers. She's not a very good sleeper and sometimes I make her a cup of tea or just sit with her and talk till she drops off again.'

'Do you go in whether she calls you or not?' Dorothy sounded suspicious.

'I generally wake myself two or three times during the night and you quickly get into a routine. If she's all right I just slip back to bed. I went in a few minutes ago, and I could see at once there was something wrong.'

'She was queer all last night,' said Dorothy slowly. 'I knew it would be too much for her, having so many people, but she insisted . . .'

'I think she had something on her mind,' Ruth confessed. 'She was a little strange in her talk . . .'

'What do you mean? What did she say?'

'She asked me twice to stay with her. I thought at first she meant for the night, but it wasn't that. She got the idea into her head that I might be going—I can't think why. I said of course I'd stay as long as she wanted me, and she said, "Don't let them drive you out." '

'What on earth did she mean by that?' Dorothy sounded scornful.

'I can't imagine, unless of course someone was urging her to do that very thing.'

'She hadn't any idea of making a change,' said Kate briskly. 'The fact is, Ruth, she was afraid you might get bored here, find it dull—after all, it's a great change for you, you're accustomed to plenty of people and parties and so forth. And then she was overtired, and things got out of perspective. That's all it was. I'll go down and ring up Dr Freeman now. Perhaps we're making a mountain out of a molehill, but he made me promise to get in touch with him if ever I became anxious.' Pulling the red dressing-gown cord about her waist, she hurried down the stairs.

Dingle Hall was old-fashioned as regards telephones. There was one instrument in the hall and an extension to the library. There were none on the upper floors. 'I go to bed to sleep,' Lady Dingle would announce flatly. 'If I'm in bed at other than the normal times it's because I'm ill. I certainly don't propose to have outsiders forcing their way into my bedroom.'

As Kate disappeared round the bend, Ruth said, 'I think I'd better go back. I don't anticipate any change, but I don't like leaving Lady Dingle alone.'

Dorothy asked abruptly, 'What woke Kate?'

'I did,' said Ruth.

'Why Kate? Why not my husband? After all, he's the obvious person.'

'I never thought of such a thing,' admitted Ruth frankly. 'Kate's been here for thirty years, and thirty years is a long time.'

'What on earth's going on?' demanded Roger's voice. His head came poking round the door. 'Is somebody dead or something?'

'Be careful,' exclaimed Dorothy. 'It's your mother. Kate thinks she's had a stroke, perhaps. She's ringing up Dr Freeman.'

Kate came back, climbing the stairs wearily. 'I've got him,' she said. 'It's an awful thing to say, but I hope we're not bringing him out for nothing. He sounds absolutely exhausted. I suppose I'd better put on a kettle or something, doctors always seem to want hot water, and, if he doesn't, it'll come in for tea.'

Ruth went back to the sick-room. Kate turned towards the stairs. Dorothy's voice halted her.

'Kate! Wait one minute. Dr Freeman can't get here for a little while. What did Mrs Appleyard mean about someone trying to drive her away?'

'I don't know,' said Kate, meeting her eyes. 'There's never been any talk of it before. I don't know if Roger . . .'

'You know perfectly well Roger's only got to give his mother a piece of advice for her to do precisely the opposite. All the same, I'm convinced she's dangerous.'

'Mrs Appleyard?'

'Yes. Kate—keep this to yourself, but—Lady Dingle's leaving her a preposterous legacy at the expense of—of others who have a far greater right.'

'Cecil?' asked Kate.

'Not only Cecil. In a way, this collapse could be called a godsend.'

'Who by?' asked Kate, bluntly and ungrammatically.

'Practically everyone, except Lady Dingle and this woman.'

'Ruth?'

'Yes. You see, she only gets the money if she's in Lady

D's employ at the time of her death—my dear mother-in-law's death, of course. Well, I don't know a great deal about strokes, but I should imagine that what's wanted now isn't a companion but a nurse. This condition may go on for ages, mayn't it?'

Kate shook her head. 'I don't know. I've never done any nursing. Dorothy, I think we should wait till the doctor's been. If he insists on a nurse . . .' she paused.

'You mean, that would simplify our position. You see, by this time next year, if she were in her right, at least her normal, mind, Lady Dingle would probably have cancelled that will and made another, more just to everyone . . .'

'Except Ruth.'

'Oh Kate!' Dorothy flung discretion to the winds. 'It's so disgracefully unfair. Here's Mrs Appleyard, virtually a stranger, being treated like a favourite daughter and the rest of us no-where. I'm convinced the situation wouldn't continue. You know how she takes likes and dislikes.'

'She's never taken to a companion before,' was Kate's dry retort. 'Of course, Ruth had the sense to stand up to her from the outset, let her see this wasn't her last chance. Miss Bennett and the others couldn't afford to quarrel with their bread-and-butter. Their market narrowed with every month. It'll be years before Ruth will have to start wondering how to pay the rent for a bed-sitting-room and spend the days in the lounges of big shops to save heat and light.'

'Is that what the others did?' Dorothy sounded shocked.

'Miss Austin—you remember her?—she was the last but one—told me she had a regular rota—Harridges one day and the Naval & Military Stores the next—she said you soon got to recognise faces . . .'

The conversation was interrupted by the appearance of Frank Hardy, who had paused to put on some clothes.

'Father Christmas is calling very early,' he suggested. 'I've just heard his car pull up.'

'The doctor,' exclaimed Kate, plunging down the stairs.

The front-door bell pealed irritably, and Kate hastened to let Dr Freeman in. He was obviously tired and his face was red with sleep.

'What is it?' he demanded.

'We think it's some sort of stroke. I do hope we haven't brought you out for nothing.'

'On the contrary, you should hope you have,' replied the doctor grimly. He came striding up the steps, two at a time, his familiar old black bag in his hand. Roger emerged from his room hurriedly, but fully dressed now. 'Hullo, Roger. Sorry to hear about your mother.' He had known them all since boyhood, had been in the neighbourhood for forty years, stepping into his father's practice when the old man died.

'It's very sudden.' Roger looked as dismayed as Frank had done.

'Strokes generally are.' He pushed his way into the big room where Ruth was standing by the bed. 'Any change?' he demanded. 'By the way, who gave the alarm? Mrs Appleyard? What roused you?'

'She didn't seem quite herself last night—anyway I usually look in in the small hours.'

'Hasn't tried to speak or anything?' He put down the bag. 'I don't want more than one of you in here. I can tell you straight away she's not going to be conscious for some time yet.' He shoo-ed them all out of the room.

'Do you want me to go?' asked Ruth.

'I'll stay,' said Kate, quickly, and Ruth went out with the rest.

She took herself down to the kitchen where, after a few minutes, Frank joined her.

'Have you come to tell me I'm responsible for this, too?' she demanded.

'You must admit that wherever you are things happen.'

'It hasn't occurred to you, I suppose,' flashed Ruth, 'that you may be the malign influence? Nothing happened to Jack till the day you appeared on the scene. Lady Dingle was perfectly all right before your arrival yesterday.'

Frank drew in his breath in a veritable hiss of admiration. 'No one will have to worry over your future,' he congratulated her. 'You think of everything.'

'You could see for yourself she was terribly wrought-up last night. I don't know what went on during that family free-for-all, but it was obvious it hadn't been a peaceful session. It would hardly have surprised me if she'd had a stroke at the bridge table. You were in the room, you . . .'

'Yes,' agreed Frank in very sober tones. Again, he saw Dorothy, trembling with resentment, heard her low, furious voice. 'I remember thinking it was hardly the Christmas spirit about which we hear so much.' And he added casually, 'What happened last night?'

'Last night? But you were there . . .'

'I don't mean downstairs. I mean after you carted the old lady up to bed.'

'Nothing unusual. I gave her a hand as I usually do. She seemed very highly strung, which is unusual for her—oh yes, it is, in the ordinary way she seems as hard as a hickory nut, but last night she seemed—almost frightened. She held my hand and told me not to let anyone drive me away.' Her voice changed abruptly. 'Don't you believe me?'

'Did she suggest who was trying to?'

'No. But you can't pretend I'm exactly *persona grata* with the Roger Dingles at least.'

'You mustn't be surprised,' he said kindly. 'The original in-habitants of the nest can't be expected to welcome the cuckoo.'

'I'm not quite sure what you're accusing me of,' confessed Ruth, 'but if they'd played their hands sensibly this situation would never have arisen.'

'People are fools,' Frank agreed. 'They don't see round corners, are unsuspecting . . . Hello, here comes the doctor. Well, he hasn't been long.'

Dr Freeman's voice carried down the back hall. 'I hope that young woman's got the kettle boiling. I could do with something hot. It's cold enough out now to freeze a brass monkey.'

He came into the kitchen followed by Roger and Dorothy, who said, 'What a Christmas morning.'

The doctor's head came round sharply. 'Christmas! So it is. I'd forgotten. Well, no reason why I should remember it speci-ally. It makes no difference to me. People die or get born or fall sick on Christmas Day as much as on any other of the

364 days of the year.' He dropped into a chair at the table saying to Ruth, 'Four lumps, please.'

Roger went away and came back with a bottle of rum. 'Have a jorum of this. Ought we to get a nurse?'

'Mrs Appleyard isn't a nurse? No? Then the answer's in the affirmative. You'll have to carry on a day or two, I shan't get anyone on Christmas Day. And these chronic cases aren't popular. There's a certain degree of paralysis down one side already; how far the brain and mind are affected I can't say definitely, how long she'll remain like a log is equally uncertain. She might come round, have a period of consciousness, recognise all or any of you, or, humanely speaking, this may be the end of her conscious life. You can't dogmatise in cases like these.'

'You can't, I suppose, give us any notion of how long ..' Roger broke off uncomfortably.

'I can't prophesy at this stage. Anything's possible, of course. I've got a chap in a private ward at St Anselm's, and I swear to you he's practically synthetic, all tubes and no functions. According to society, it's my duty to keep the poor devil breathing; if I used my common sense and let him go, I'd be guilty of negligence, probably criminal negligence, at the very least. Upon my sam, we live in a lunatic world and if we don't behave like lunatics ourselves we're locked up—in asylums or gaols.' He held out his cup to Ruth. 'That's the way I like my tea,' he said, 'so that you can float a hen on it.'

Dorothy looked up sharply. 'I expect Kate would like a cup,' she observed.

'I was just going to take her one,' agreed Ruth, unruffled. She filled a cup and carried it out of the room.

'Lady Dingle was lucky getting that young woman,' remarked the doctor, as the door closed.

'There won't be anything for her to do now,' objected Roger. 'You've made it perfectly clear that, so far as any social life is concerned, my mother's turn is over.'

'She's fond of Mrs Appleyard,' insisted Dr Freeman. 'She's told me so more than once. That other poor old girl you had— what was her name? Benson or something—Lady Dingle told me it was like biting into a soft apple trying to talk to her, whereas this girl is as crisp as a pippin. Still, you're right, Roger. I've always been against the sacrifice of youth to old age and sickness. That girl shouldn't be allowed to moulder here, once the household's got into its swing. What's her story? Widow?'

'Her husband was killed in a car accident abroad,' said Frank, when no one else replied.

'Bad luck. Still, I doubt if she wears her weeds to her grave.' He pushed back his cup and got to his feet. 'I must be getting along. Mrs Curtis down by the bridge has been expecting her baby for the past ten days. I never knew such an unpunctual woman. Not that she cares. "I wanted it to come on Christmas Day," she croons, the great gaby. Doesn't give a thought to the doctor's convenience, of course. I'll look in again tonight or in the morning.' He turned at the door. 'Take my advice and don't let this upset your whole day. There's nothing you can do for the old lady except just keep an eye on her, of course. You won't do anyone any good sitting around and moping. So eat the turkey your good Kate will cook for you and—Roger, you look all in. Overdoing it in that infernal city of Mansoul, I suppose. Well, you've got two or three days' break. Make the most of them.'

Kate was on her knees making up the fire in the sick-room. 'Tea!' she exclaimed. 'Just what I wanted. It seems to have gone cold.' She shivered. 'Is the doctor still here?'

'He's drinking tea in the kitchen.' Ruth repeated the gist of Freeman's remarks.

'I can hold the fort while you look after the dinner,' she offered. 'It's a sinecure, really, because there'll be practically nothing to be done.'

'So we're to have a nurse,' Kate frowned. 'I suppose the doctor's right, but they always seem to make trouble in a house. For one thing, servants don't like them. Well, I suppose she'll hardly affect Mrs Gusset and Mrs Gamp, but you never can tell. Sickness puts them out in any case, though actually it won't make any difference to them.'

'They won't be here for a couple of days,' Ruth reminded her, for, naturally, both these independent creatures had their own households to consider during the holiday, 'and it's even possible the nurse may be established by their return.'

'It'll be a soft job for her,' muttered Kate.

Ruth looked surprised. 'Why do you say that? These helpless cases make heavy work, lifting and so forth, and Lady Dingle won't be able to help herself. I can go on with night duty such as it is,' she added. 'I'm used to coming in and she won't want much in her present state. But if she should suddenly come round she won't want to find strangers at her bedside. You know how she is.'

'We don't know that she will come round or, if she does, how far she'll be able to recognise anyone,' said Kate grimly. 'I've seen something of strokes. A great-aunt of mine died of one. She was senile for nearly two years.'

'Don't.' Ruth's voice held a note in it that made Kate turn quickly. 'She's always been so alert, Lady Dingle, I mean, it's awful to think of her lying like a log.' She went over to the bed. 'Even now, you know, she may realise more than we guess. Even doctors can't be sure. And—it's only an idea, of course—but if she has people round her to whom she's more than just a case, it might be possible—mightn't it?—for some sort of telepathy to operate, she might feel, if she didn't actually know, that there was—affection—'

Kate stood up. 'That sounds remarkably like wishful thinking to me. The kindest thing to hope is that she doesn't know anything of the sort, that it's like a deep sleep . . .'

The feet of the Roger Dingles were heard on the stairs and she went out to meet them. Ruth brought a blanket from her own room and lay down on the sofa at the foot of the unconscious woman's bed. Nothing to be done, of course, Kate was right, but she couldn't leave her alone. Illogical, no doubt, but logic isn't always the last word.

9

When Kate come downstairs a couple of hours later she found that Frank had already brought in coal and wood and got the morning-room fire alight.

'You must let me earn my Christmas dinner,' he pointed out. 'I asked Roger if he would like me to clear out but he said no. So—will you accept me for your scullion, Kate? You don't expect me to call you Miss Waring, do you? I know we only met yesterday, but so much has happened . . .'

'Have you any experience?' murmured Kate.

'You should ask my mother.' He followed her into the kitchen. 'What would you like me to do? Clean the floor, peel the vegetables.' He looked round. 'You know, you shouldn't wear yourself out with this old-fashioned gear. In my country . . .'

'You press a button and the potatoes peel themselves. I know. If you'd told Lady Dingle that she'd have said it's no wonder we're becoming a world of robots, where no one dreams of working his fingers to the bone.'

'She should talk,' murmured Frank irreverently. 'Anyway, why should they? Come to that, have you ever seen anyone who's fingers were worked to the bone?'

'You talk a lot of nonsense,' Kate rebuked him, but some while later she heard herself say, 'You at least need never starve. People would snap you up, and you could name your own price. I begin to think there's something to be said for domestic equality between the sexes. Roger and Cecil are so ham-handed in a kitchen . . .'

'Cecil won't be, not after a few months with Vi,' Frank prophesied. 'Kate, what are you thinking?' he added a few minutes later.

Kate came to with a start. 'I was wondering how old you are.'

'Twenty-four. Why?'

'I'm old enough to be your mother. Your mother now, I suppose she's travelled a good deal.'

'Oh, she gets around,' agreed Frank, casually. 'She took me to Canada when the war broke out and my father went to France—and didn't come back. She's never come home since. She met my stepfather there and married him in '46.'

'Have you any stepbrothers or sisters?'

'One sister, aged seven.' He put his hand in his pocket and pulled out a wallet. 'Want to see her picture? Cute, isn't she?'

An impudent little face, crowned with curls, looked up at Kate. 'She looks sweet,' murmured the woman who'd had nothing, handing the picture back. Her old sense of frustration flooded her afresh. One woman had two husbands, two children, travel, friends, security, a full life, and another of about the same age had nothing but thirty years' subordination to look back upon. The contrast was too cruel.

As though he sensed her thoughts, Frank changed the conversation, and quite soon the kitchen rang with laughter. But the gaiety of the house was confined to these four walls. In the morning-room, where the Roger Dingles warmed themselves by Frank's roaring fire, the day limped by as cheerless as a beggar in a morality play. Roger had telephoned Cecil and Isobel. Cecil said he and Vi would be up to lunch, as arranged, there was no point in his coming earlier and Vi wanted him to take her to church. Isobel said she didn't want to spoil the boys' Christmas, seeing there was nothing she could do, but in the New Year, when they would be staying with school-friends, she and Hugh Exeter (her husband) would come over. Roger promised to ring up again if there was any change. Ruth spent the morning upstairs. There was plenty of work with so many guests, though she was pleased to find that Frank had left his room like a new pin. Dorothy came up while she was making the big double bed.

'You shouldn't have bothered,' she said, rather ungraciously.

'I've nothing else to do, and Lady Dingle doesn't want me,' Ruth pointed out.

The sky was as hard as iron, the wind like a knife. There was no point going out to be chilled to the bone. Ruth had performed the essential sick-room services.

'Have you done any nursing?' Dorothy demanded.

'Not this kind. But I can manage. I'm very strong and she's not too much of a weight.'

Dorothy hung about for a few minutes and then went down again. She switched on the wireless, and clear voices rang out singing *O Little Town of Bethlehem.* She turned it off again. That kind of innocence seemed to belong to a world she had left behind her long ago.

Cecil and his wife arrived at lunch-time and they all sat down to the traditional turkey and trimmings, but the entrancing Christmas tree, decked with such loving, in Kate's case almost such fanatical, care, remained in the library, its candles unlit, its tinsel tarnishing in the cold air. Violet suggested it might be taken down and given to some village household. 'Heaps of the families can't afford trees at all,' she said. She was regarded by the Dingles as *'nouveau riche,'* upstart—no, not even that, there wasn't a great deal of money, certainly not enough to justify such a title—but she knew far more about the villagers than even Cecil.

'We can't do that,' exclaimed Kate, aghast.

'But if we're not going to use it . . .'

'You don't understand. They'd break the ornaments.'

'Even if they did smash one or two you can buy more. It's not like the days after the war . . .'

'But these are old, they're traditional.'

Violet shrugged her neat shoulders. 'I don't understand how Christmas tree ornaments can be traditional. I should have thought it was much more important for some kids to have a good time . . .'

'I told you you didn't understand,' said Kate.

Later in the day Violet went upstairs to her mother-in-law's room. Ruth glanced up as the door opened softly.

'Would you like me to take a turn?' asked Violet. 'She won't know the difference . . .'

'I'm not tired,' said Ruth, 'but stay with me a little. How are things going?'

'I'll be charitable and assume it's the shock that's affected everything. Honestly, Ruth, I never saw such a family. Thank goodness when our children are old enough to appreciate Christmas there won't be a mother-in-law . . . Doris is quite different.' Doris was her stepmother, and only ten years older than Violet.

'Be careful.' The words sprang instinctively to Ruth's lips.

'Why? She can't hear, can she? I say, Ruth, you know that bit in the Bible about the proud man taking heed lest he fall— I never liked her but it must be awful for her now, if she knows anything. Let's hope she doesn't. To lie like a log and be stared at. Will she last long, do you think?'

'Dr Freeman's coming in again this afternoon. I believe people can go on for weeks and months . . . I don't think she knows anything.'

'You don't think, I don't think, Dr Freeman doesn't think, but nobody knows. I always thought I'd like to see her brought low, she's been so beastly to Cecil. He'd have married long ago but for her. Well, of course, that's a bit of luck for me. Oh yes, I know everyone thinks I jumped at the chance of marrying above me, as my mother-in-law says, but she cheated him of being young and what I know and she doesn't is that the young Cecil is still there. Like that boy who fell down the glacier and whose body was found thirty years afterwards perfect, preserved by the ice.' She paused, her fine fair brows lifted. 'It must be the champagne,' she said frankly. 'Did you get any? It's loosed the string of my tongue. And to you of all people. I mean, a widow and so forth. But the fact is, you're the only person in this house, except Cecil of course, who knows what being in love is like. Dorothy isn't in love with Roger, if she ever was. Oh Ruth, I hope when I'm dead to love I die to everything else, too. I couldn't bear to go on living for years in the dark.'

On the 28th December Dr Freeman told Roger he'd found a nurse to take over the case.

'You don't want more than one, not at present, anyhow. You've got Kate and there's Mrs Appleyard . . . I understand she's excellent in the sickroom.'

Dorothy, who was present, bit her lip. She had tried to

take her turn, but it hadn't been a success. She was too nervous of the old woman, couldn't persuade herself she wasn't being watched, she dropped things, became flustered, yet resented Ruth's success in the same role.

'It's always the same,' said Dr Freeman bluntly. 'Relations are the worst possible people in a sick-room. Not their fault. What's wanted is a competent personality and how in heaven's name can relations provide that?'

Nurse Alexander was a well-built woman in her fifties. She told the household briskly that they needn't worry now, she was there to take over and save them from that. Dorothy took an instant dislike to her, Kate said she looked capable, Isobel, who had just arrived with her husband, hoped she'd stay. Nobody asked Ruth what she thought. Roger and Dorothy were still on the premises, and so was Frank Hardy. 'For goodness' sake, stay,' Dorothy implored him. 'This place is like the morgue and Kate says you're invaluable. We've got to hang on till Mr Holles comes down. Apparently he went to Austria for Christmas and isn't expected back till the end of next week. Mamma-in-law was always cagey about her affairs and he's more in her confidence than anyone else. Roger wants him to come down here and see the set-up for himself,' she added, seeing a slightly puzzled look on her companion's face. 'If there's not likely to be any change and this condition goes on indefinitely he may suggest shutting up the house—one of the so-called helps has already handed in her notice—she says she never could abide nurses and it brings everything back, whatever that may mean —anyway, we'll get his advice.'

'What'll happen to Kate if Lady Dingle goes into a nursing-home, which, I suppose, is what you mean?'

'I think you can safely leave that to Roger,' said Dorothy, with a touch of stiffness. 'Naturally Mrs Appleyard could find herself another job without difficulty.

'Have you told her?'

'No. And I hope you won't say anything about it. We can't do anything till we've seen Mr Holles. It's only a few more days, and Roger has nothing very pressing in London.'

What they meant, of course, as Frank knew, was that they didn't propose to shift and leave Ruth in part possession. More, if they could get Ruth out during the old woman's lifetime, they'd save her legacy.

Violet, however, considered herself bound by no such scruple. When she found herself alone with Ruth she said, 'I suppose you know what Roger and co. are after. They're going to persuade old Holles that you're—what's the word?—redundant. He may not agree, but—I thought you ought to know.'

'I appreciate it,' said Ruth thoughtfully. 'Does your husband . . .?'

'Know? or agree? I carefully haven't asked him. He has trouble enough with his frightful family without me making it any worse. You know, Lady D. thought it was no end of a come-down for her son to marry a farmer's daughter, but she never stopped to think that it's not all to the cream puffs marrying into her crowd. I never knew such a gang, schemers to a man. I thought you ought to be on your guard. People like that have to be heard to be believed.'

Ruth asked, 'When is Mr Holles expected?'

'Within the week, I gather. Let's hope he has some decent feelings, but—I doubt it. No lawyer with decent feelings would have tied himself up with this lot. I've been talking to Frank. If things fold up here as they may, I want to take Cecil and Dingle Junior to Canada. It's all nonsense about Cecil being too old. Nobody's ever too old for anything, until they think they are.'

Ruth went up to her room and lay down on her bed, brooding on what she'd just heard. She didn't for a moment doubt the truth of what Violet had told her. Of course the Dingles would try and oust her before it was too late. So, reflected Ruth sensibly, would a great many other people. She wasn't sure of her legal position, but she didn't feel like pinning too much faith on that. She wondered how much Lady Dingle had got her down for—something handsome, obviously, or they wouldn't be plotting with such haste.

Steps sounded outside and Nurse poked her head in.

'I'm going down to get a cup of tea,' she said, looking as fresh as a daisy in contrast to Ruth, whose hair was tumbled and face pale. 'You might look in on my patient, there's a dear. No hurry; she's not likely to move for days, poor creature, if ever, but these people are what I call amateurs in illness, everything frightens them into fits. Like a mother with her first child. Little darling coughs and she knows it'll be dead of convulsions by morning, so off with the telephone and out with the doctor and presently she's all beams, it's perfectly well, you have taken a load off my mind, I always say you can't be too careful . . .'

She went heartily down the stairs, and Ruth brushed her hair to its accustomed neatness, powdered her face, found her shoes and went quietly along to the sick woman's room. There was a comfortable chair with a fat buttoned green cushion, standing in the corner of the room. Lady Dingle lay like a lump against her pillows.

Ruth came to stand beside the bed. 'Do you know anything of what's going on?' she asked softly, bending above that pale unresponsive face. 'Can you make any sign, let me know if you realise there's someone here? Look.' She snatched up the green cushion and returned to the bed. 'Now.' Suddenly she let the cushion fall. There was no response whatsoever from the bed's inmate, not so much as a flicker of the eyes. 'No,' said Ruth in the same soft voice, 'you don't see or you'd have glanced down as one does instinctively when something drops.' She touched the hand. It seemed quite nerveless. 'Where are you now?' she wondered. 'Out of your senses, they say, but you must be somewhere. Where? And can you still think in that province beyond our knowledge?' She picked up the cushion again.

The door opened suddenly and Dorothy came in. 'Mrs Appleyard, what are you doing with that cushion?'

'An experiment,' said Ruth, returning it to the armchair. 'I hoped she might make some sign—'

'You know she can't.' Dorothy sounded both angry and contemptuous. 'It's cruel—'

'If she can't see me—or hear me—what harm can I do? I was watching her eyes—but they never moved. How little we know really,' she went on. 'Her mind may be as keen as yours or mine, but because her body's failed she can't give us the smallest indication. It's like being imprisoned in a room with all the curtains drawn. Darkness everywhere.' She shivered for a moment, though the room was warm enough.

'Oh, I don't suppose she knows anything. One thing, she's not in any pain.'

'No? There's mental suffering—*The Nightmare Life-in-Death is She, Who thicks men's blood with cold.*'

Dorothy said firmly. 'Poetry? It doesn't do to give your imagination too much play, Mrs Appleyard. I'm going to sit with Lady Dingle for a little while. Why don't you go down and get a cup of tea?'

Their eyes met. Here was the challenge thrown down with a vengeance. There's no place for you here. Keep out. That was what Dorothy meant. Ruth met that implacable gaze, smiled suddenly and said, 'That's very thoughtful of you, Mrs Dingle. I'll slip down and when I've had it I'll relieve you up here.'

'Don't hurry,' said Dorothy, distinctly. 'I've brought my knitting and I shall hold the fort till Nurse Alexander returns.'

In the kitchen it was warm and cosy. Kate poured out the tea. 'Is Ruth with Lady Dingle?' she asked. 'I'll make her a fresh cup when she comes down.'

'Make these scones yourself?' asked Nurse keenly. She liked her food and throve on it. 'You're wasted here, my dear. I know cooks getting six pounds a week all found and they're not a patch on you.' She took another. 'That Mrs Appleyard. I don't seem quite to fit her into the picture. Is she another relation?'

'Oh no,' Kate explained. 'She's Lady Dingle's companion. Or has been for the past six months.'

'There's another who's wasting her time,' Nurse continued. She liked to say she called a spade a spade. 'A girl with her looks—living apart from her husband, I suppose?'

'Mrs Appleyard is a widow.' Kate began to take a dislike to Nurse Alexander.

'Left badly off? Well, obviously, or she wouldn't take a job like this. Not much for her down here, I should have thought. Still,' she took another scone, 'no doubt she has her reasons.' Tranquilly she abandoned the subject of Ruth. 'Poor old lady! Let's hope she gets her call soon. Always been very active, I understand.'

Her eyes, small and round and black, suddenly put Kate

in mind of a mouse. She wasn't a weak-minded woman, she told herself, but a mouse could still make her shudder. Suddenly she wished herself in London, Australia, Timbuktu, anywhere out of this house where she'd lived so long and known so much wretchedness. There had been pleasure and tranquillity, too, of course, but at the moment only the dark periods were clear in her memory.

Roger displayed some subtlety in dealing with the problem of Ruth's £10,000. He said nothing direct to the girl, and a day or so later went up to London for a night to deal, he said, with a number of outstanding matters. On his return he suggested to the doctor that he and his brother would be happier if Lady Dingle had trained attendants night and day. 'In that case, we could release Mrs Appleyard, who was never engaged for this sort of work,' he said. He knew about the difficulty of getting nurses for this kind of unrewarding case, but he had heard of a retired nurse named Mortimer, who sometimes went out and who, he had been given to understand, might be prepared to lend a hand. The following day he reported he had been in touch with Nurse Mortimer who was on a case as relief-nurse at the moment, but could be available in about a fortnight.

'You'll need to give Mrs Appleyard some kind of notice,' Freeman pointed out, 'so that should suit very well.'

That evening Roger summoned Ruth to the library and explained the new development. Ruth said nothing. Roger went on, a little clumsily, 'I should like to thank you for being so helpful since my mother's collapse and, of course, for everything you did for her before that time. I hope you'll allow us to make you some small return of a financial nature. I believe,' he added hurriedly, 'it was my mother's intention to mention you in her will. I intend to honour that intention.'

Ruth's blue eyes opened wide. 'You're very generous, Mr Dingle.'

'You have been here less than a year, I understand. I propose to make you an ex gratia payment of one hundred pounds over and above your month's salary.'

'May I ask you something?' asked Ruth.

'What is that, Mrs Appleyard?'

'How does that compare with the provision Lady Dingle made for me in the will she drew up recently?'

'If my mother allowed you to suppose that any such provision would accrue in any circumstances, I am afraid she misled you. She was anticipating many years of your services, but naturally there's no niche for you in this household any longer. The legacy would only come to you if you were still in her employ, which in the nature of things is no longer possible.'

'Probable,' corrected Ruth, gently. 'How fortunate for you, Mr Dingle, that your mother didn't collapse at once after her stroke, as she so easily might have done. Would it be impertinent to ask how much I'm down for in the last will?'

'I haven't seen it,' said Roger coldly, 'and yes, I do consider it impertinent. Under that will you would only receive a legacy if you were still at Dingle Hall. I am proposing to make you a present of a hundred pounds under no legal compulsion whatsoever. As for the amount, if I had considered it disproportionate, I should most certainly have contested the will on the family's behalf. There are unpleasant words for young women who exercise undue influence on old ones.'

'I didn't influence her at all,' said Ruth, steadily. 'And I suppose she was at liberty to do what she pleased with her money.'

'That is a moot point. I have been making a few enquiries about you, Mrs Appleyard. I believe this is your first employment as a companion?'

'When I was married I didn't need to work. I had a husband . . .'

'Precisely. And before your marriage you lived in London with a Mrs Martin?'

'Well?'

'Your name was then Ruth Garside. Shall I go on? You do appreciate that in any court proceedings these facts would be bound to emerge?'

'I see no reason for it,' said Ruth. 'They don't affect the present case.' She added, 'If I may ask a second question, what exactly is the relationship between Mr Hardy and yourself?'

'I don't understand you.'

'Oh, I know the source of your information,' she cried, scornfully.

Roger looked amazed. 'You mean, he knew?'

'Naturally, I realise that he told you. I ought to have guessed.'

'You are wrong,' said Roger, tight-lipped, turning rather pale. 'Frank Hardy said nothing to me. In the circumstances, I consider that most reprehensible. If he knew as much as I know now, it should have been obvious to him that you were no suitable person to have charge of a helpless elderly woman, from whose death you would hope to reap a considerable benefit.'

'Would you like to repeat that in front of a lawyer?' demanded Ruth, also going white.

Roger realised he had gone too far, but he wouldn't step back. 'I have to think of my mother,' he said in his most pompous fashion.

'Oh nonsense,' retorted Ruth. 'You're thinking of the money, first, last and all the time. But don't count your chickens before they're hatched, Mr Dingle.' And she added rashly, 'I have a lawyer, too.'

Walking round the garden, because she needed air, after that difficult interview, she caught sight of Frank Hardy standing at one of the upper windows. Instantly she clenched her hands and shook them above her head in the comrades salute. Frank stared, turned away and a minute later joined her in the garden.

'What did that pantomime mean?' he demanded.

'You can't guess, of course.' She laughed angrily. 'Oh, excellent young man! So conscience won, after all. You felt you must be a good citizen and do your duty so you went running to Roger Dingle—or perhaps that was part of your conception of singing for your supper.'

Frank was as angry as she. He caught her arm and shook it till she said with suppressed rage, 'I shall be black and blue tomorrow.'

'I'm sorry it's only your arm,' said Frank. 'What did you mean by what you said?'

'Are you going to ask me to believe at this stage that you

never breathed a word to either of the Dingles about—Ruth Garside?'

He whistled, a low clear note. 'So that cat's out of the bag? Well, I didn't untie the string, but, all things considered, I think you might be thankful to whoever did. Oh, can't you see anythink but the money, Ruth? Of course it would be jolly to have a legacy and be independent and so forth, though candidly I think you're counting chickens before they're hatched if you think that last will would go through without protest from the family, but how will that help you if Lady Dingle should die suddenly, in the night, say, when you're nominally in charge, and it comes out that you inherit a small fortune?'

'You know perfectly well she might be dying at this minute while I'm talking to you in the garden. Would you still hold me responsible?'

'It isn't what I think. It's what people in general might say. Ten thousand pounds is a good deal of money . . .'

'Ten thousand pounds! Is that what she meant me to have? I can't believe it. I never dreamed.' She laughed again. 'Dear Mr Frank Hardy, do you really think I'd let that amount go for a mere hundred pounds, which is what Roger Dingle offered me for going quietly, just to satisfy some scruple of yours?'

'I can see I'm wasting my time,' agreed Frank.

'Just one more question. Why are you taking so much interest in my affairs?'

'I can only think of one answer that fits the bill and that is that you've got under my skin, Ruth Appleyard. And it couldn't be that, could it? Only—I told you I believe in a pattern, and it hasn't worked itself out yet.'

After some thought Ruth wrote to Mr Devenish, but a few days later, and on the eve of Mr Holles's expected arrival at Dingle Hall, an answer came back from Grace Devenish to the effect that her husband had entered hospital for an operation and wouldn't be available to his clients for at least six weeks.

10

The calendar stood at January 6th. Nurse Alexander stood beside her patient's bed; the green cushion in the little chair bore the imprint of her sturdy figure.

'Twelfth Night,' said Nurse, with a sigh for the merry days of youth in her native land and the fun, the dancing, the games; and afterwards, telling fortunes round the big kitchen table by lamplight to see who'd get a wedding-ring before next Twelfth Night, and secret reflections among the old as to which would have earned a shroud. It seemed a very long time ago—nearly forty years—the whole world had turned topsy-turvy in that time.

'How much you must remember,' Nurse apostrophised her unconscious charge. 'Pity you can't talk. Wonder if you ever will come out of that darkness. Better for you, I dare say, if you don't. You'll never be much more than a log for the rest of your days. Ah well, seventy-four's a good age and by all accounts you've had a handsome run for your money.'

She went over to make up the fire. The room was warm, but once the coals dimmed it had a clammy feeling. There was a heaviness in the atmosphere this afternoon, as though a storm was planning to creep up and take them unawares. 'Shouldn't be surprised if we have thunder,' announced Nurse, laying down the poker. She hoped not. Thunder always gave her a headache. Ruth Appleyard seemed similarly affected. She had complained that morning of migraine and had gone to lie down with the curtains drawn, saying she'd take a tablet and hoped to be able to come on duty in the afternoon as usual. Isobel had taken over for her at lunch-time, and afterwards had gone for a walk with young Frank Hardy. Nurse thought about Frank for a bit—she was a born romantic and loved weaving dreams about young men and women—that Mrs Appleyard now? was

Frank attracted? She'd come upon them more than once chatting together in corners—then her thoughts passed on to the other members of the household. You might have expected one of the others would offer to come up at tea-time— Dorothy, say. Still, she was a peril in any sickroom—'shouldn't like to be her husband when he's ill,' reflected Nurse. And Kate, of course, would be busy with the tea. That lawyer of theirs was expected next day and Isobel was staying till he arrived, though her husband, sensible chap, had gone back to London. Nurse wondered how long the rest of the family meant to hang on.

'Sad, really,' reflected Nurse, coming back to the bedside, 'so much money and so little love.' But in the novels she liked best they hardly ever did go together.

3.45 at last. She opened the door of the sickroom and stared out to the dark landing. No one about or the light would be on already, an afternoon like this. She pressed the switch, and there was a flicker, a glow, and then darkness again. Bulb gone. Nurse sighed. Another little job for Kate. She left the invalid's door a little ajar to catch a ray from the bedside lamp that never went out. She walked along to Ruth's room, tapped on the door and then opened it.

'Wakey, wakey,' she called in her humorous way.

She could just make out a dark figure on the bed. A shame to disturb her really, but there it was. The family wouldn't see why they shouldn't get their money's worth out of an employee. Trust Roger Dingle for that. It was generally the rich, in her experience, who were careful about tips, waited for the last halfpenny of their change.

One thing, she told herself cosily, there was always plenty of hot water. If she was very quick she might be able to fit in a bath. No one else was likely to want one this hour of the day. And Kate wouldn't complain if she was a few minutes late for once. She turned on the tap and the water came gushing out, the steam rose. Back in her room, putting on her dressing-gown, she heard Lady Dingle's door close with its familiar creak. She peeped out. Ruth's door was now shut. Must be feeling better. That was a comfort. She picked up her green towel and the pretty plastic sponge bag that had been a gift from her last patient and came on to the landing. Voices floated up from the hall. Roger—and Cecil. In and out like a jack-in-the-box, she reflected. Devoted sons—she grinned wryly—not staying to tea, though, by the sound of it, or coming up to see his mother. Not that it 'ud make any difference if he did, but it would have been a nice gesture.

'I wish I could meet your request,' Roger was saying with his usual worried inflection. 'The fact is, I'm practically in Queer Street myself. I'd hoped to enlist Mother's sympathies, but . . .'

'I'll have a word with Holles,' said Cecil. 'It ought to be possible to come to some arrangement now Mother's in this condition.'

'We need a power of attorney, but she's in no state to execute one. Still, there's a chance she might have a period of consciousness. He'll be able to tackle Mrs Appleyard, too. With Nurse Mortimer coming on Monday there's no point in Mrs Appleyard stopping on.'

Nurse Alexander grimaced and went into the bathroom. No one had consulted her about Nurse Mortimer. The two women had met before, and each believed the other to be an autocrat. 'I prefer to work single-handed,' Mortimer always said. 'Well, there's one thing we've got in common,' Nurse Alexander observed to no one in particular. 'If that woman's going to stay long I shall look for some other patient.' She thought about the brothers and the snatch of conversation she had overheard. 'Best news either of them could have would be to hear the old lady's passed on. But seeing she's been disobliging all her life, from what I can gather, she's not likely to change now. Death-bed repentances,' reflected Nurse, popping into the hot water. 'I've seen plenty of death-beds and I could count the repentances on the fingers of one hand. For one thing, they're mostly past it when they get to that stage. Oh well, no sense meeting trouble half-way.' She lifted up a not very tuneful voice and began to sing:

'If I were the only girl in the world and you were the only boy . . .'

There wasn't much light in the sickroom, a tongue of flame from the fire Nurse had just made up and a glow from the shaded bedside lamp. The heavy furniture, the old-fashioned ornaments, the dark curtains at the windows, all these were in shadow. The old woman opened her eyes. She felt confused, slowly recognised nearby objects with the queer sensation that somehow they had nothing more to do with her. It was like being in a train that's entered a long tunnel. Now it was drawing out into the evening light but what country it had passed through in the tunnel, that you could never be sure about.

She tried to move her hand, but it seemed as if someone had filled it with lead. She opened her mouth but the words wouldn't come out. Someone had taken a key and locked all her limbs; her features, even her thoughts, were stiff as an unoiled gate. The head moved an inch or so and a now familiar face bent over hers.

'What is it?'

The words she thought she said came as no more than a gasp to the listener's ear.

'Can you hear me? See? Understand?'

But no expression stirred in that mask of sharpened bone and dry polished skin. The bed and its fearful occupant reeked of death; corruption hung on the choked air.

'Ruth.'

'What are you trying to say? Save yourself the trouble, there's nothing you can do.'

Dramatically, with a macabre effect, a bell tolled a long way off, the single notes following each other with a harsh monotony. One and one and one and one and one . . . The death bell.

From the bed came another gasp. Will? Was that it? Something about the will. Ruth. The will. Or was that fancy? It might have been 'ill.' 'Am I ill?'

'Yes. You're ill. Lie quiet. Don't try to speak.'

Sense stole back into the eyes, that implored, the fingers of the immobilised hand stirred with a faint plucking movement. Somewhere behind the portico of bone a light had been kindled, the merest glow that a breeze could extinguish, a mere puff of air.

The mouth opened wider. Breath quickened.

'What is it?' The sound that emerged was no stronger than a bat's cry. But even a bat's cry was too loud.

'Hush!' A hand covered her mouth. 'Can't you understand? It's too late.'

The fingers worked a little faster, pleating the coverlet. This, then, was what Dr Freeman had prophesied, a period of consciousness, long enough perhaps to undo an injustice, to wreck hope . . . The hand that didn't cover the dry lips stretched out, took up the green cushion. There was an instant of darkness as its bulk came between lamp and bed. The eyes closed—in fear? acceptance? Who could say?

It needed such a little effort, such a little time. When you're almost through the door of death it requires only the faintest push to complete the entry, just a minute's darkness, no time to suffer or understand. 'You'd thank me if you knew, saving you all the months ahead. You hate illness, helplessness. Do you remember telling me how you never would say that verse in the litany from battle, murder and sudden death, deliver us, Good Lord? You always said sudden death was a blessing, a blessing . . .'

It was over now, the cushion had been hurled back into the armchair, there wasn't a sound. Now quick, decide what to do next. Be shocked? relieved? Say—no, I didn't go in, I didn't know, she must have died in her sleep. Or—run down the stairs, raise the alarm. 'Nurse Alexander, where's Nurse Alexander? Nurse, I think you ought to come, there's been a change?' Which? Which?

Murder glanced down at the bed and a ghastly thing happened. The closed eyes were opening. 'No,' whispered Murder in horror. But it didn't mean anything, was simply a physical reaction, the relaxation of the muscles—in the same way that a hen whose head is chopped off will go running a few paces before she drops. All the same, it was uncanny, not to be endured.

Murder put out a shaking hand and switched off the light.

Isobel and Frank had not got very far when Frank said, 'Thunder on the way. I can smell it. What now?'

'We go home,' said Isobel firmly. 'I'm not precisely made

of sugar, but there's no sense being caught in a thunderstorm in the open.'

As they reached the gate they met Cecil coming away. Isobel stopped to talk to him. Frank went in by the back door. The imminent thunder seemed to have got inside the house; it had a sinister atmosphere. No social life seemed to be stirring, so presently he went along to the billiard room and began to knock the balls about.

In the bathroom Nurse sang gallantly:

> 'A garden of Eden just made for two,
> With nothing to mar our joy.'

Kate heard her as she came out of her room. The landing light wouldn't work and all the doors seemed to be shut. She made her way over to the back stairs, wondered, 'Shall I take a peep at the old lady? No, late already,' and hurried down. Fortunately on the lower floor you couldn't hear the singing. What Lady Dingle would say at the picture of Nurse shouting her amorous hopes to a houseful of strangers she couldn't imagine. Sir John had never sung in his bath, never had the spirit, poor creature. Nurse now would sing at a graveside. Kate had a vision of her burying her late patient and yelling:

> 'When our hearts are filled with woe.'

She put the kettle on and began to take down the cups from the dresser.

Nurse came down a little later in the brightest of moods. 'I will say one thing for you,' she announced, 'you don't stint the coke. I've been in houses where there wasn't any hot water except at morning and night. No scones today? (The creature dearly loved her food.) Well, currant bread makes a change. This one of your cakes? Scrumptious. Some poor man was done out of a good wife when you decided to stay single. Still, many a good tune played on an old fiddle, and we may see you

wearing orange-blossoms yet. I'll be your matron of honour.'
She roared at her own facetiousness.

Kate's glance was like the north wind. Her voice matched
it.

'How's Mrs Appleyard's head?' she enquired. 'Is she with
Lady Dingle?'

'Better, I suppose,' said Nurse cheerfully, her mouth full of
cake. 'I've got a bit of a headache myself. Thunder in the air.
Yes, I heard her go in. Talking of orange-blossoms, do you think
there might be anything between her and that young Hardy?'
Kate was speechless. 'What's his job anyway?' continued Nurse,
supremely innocent of offence. 'Whatever it is it seems to give
him plenty of time off. Writer p'raps.' She held out her cup to
be refilled. 'I've often thought with what I've learnt in other
people's houses I might write a book myself one of these days.
Crimes at the Clinic. Catchy title, don't you think? Or here's
another idea. The Doctor's Name was Death. Bit long p'raps.'
She brooded.

'You old vulture,' thought Kate, and the teapot shook in her
hand. 'You jackal, I believe you'd write a penny dreadful round
us tomorrow if you knew how.'

A man's step came purposefully down the passage and Frank
Hardy stuck his head round the door.

'Hullo, Kate! Commissariat gone on strike? Or could you do
with a manly arm?'

'I was waiting for you and Isobel to come back,' said Kate,
taking down the best teapot and pouring in a little water from
the big kettle on the stove.

'Kate—dear! We've been back ages. We smelt thunder. Isobel
met Cecil at the gate . . .'

'Cecil! Has he been here?'

'It seems so. Anyway, I left them talking and since there
didn't seem to be any life stirring and it was too early for tea
I wandered along to pot a few balls in the billiard-room. Quite
fun,' he added, 'like playing an obstacle race, with all those
cuts in the cloth.'

'That was the boys last year. Roger was rather put out about
it, but Lady Dingle said she wasn't going to pay for a new
cloth, and no one ever used the table anyhow.'

The door flashed open. Dorothy appeared on the threshold. 'Nurse, what's the meaning of this? Why is my mother-in-law left alone? I thought Mrs Appleyard . . .'

Nurse thought, 'Of all the sauce! Trying to teach me my job,' but she only said quite coolly, 'Isn't she in with the old lady? Well, I dare say she's just gone out of the room for a sec. The best of us are subject to the demands of nature. She's probably back by this time.'

'It won't make much difference if she's there or not—now.' Dorothy stared at the three faces all turned to hers and stood her ground.

'If you've finished your tea, Nurse . . . It was just chance that I looked in. I've been up in the attics, there was something I wanted. I noticed there was no light under the door. There's no light on the landing either.'

'I know,' said Kate. 'I have got a new one out. I'll put it in after tea.'

'I think it's dreadful.' Dorothy's voice rose. Wait for it, thought Nurse. Hysterics any minute now. 'Leaving her alone in the dark to die in a houseful of people . . .'

If she expected Nurse to look conscience-stricken or display uneasiness she was disappointed. Nurse refastened her cuffs, tied on her apron.

'Now, keep your calm, Mrs Dingle,' she said in authoritative tones. 'If the old lady really has passed on, that's nothing to shed tears about. None of us would want to lie week in, week out, like a log. She was lucky really to go so easily.'

'How do you know it was easy? You weren't there.'

Kate said sharply, 'Does Roger know?'

'I'm just going to tell him.' She dashed away.

'If Mrs Roger isn't careful,' remarked Nurse, picking up her cup and draining the last drop of tea, 'she's going to be a nervous case. I must say I never thought there was much love lost between those two. And nothing to shed tears over anyway. Poor old thing!'

She marched upstairs, expecting to find Ruth in the sickroom, but there was no one there. The central light was burning and the little bedside lamp had been extinguished. She realised immediately that Dorothy hadn't exaggerated the facts. Death had left his card here all right. The sound of feet on the stairs brought a frown to her face. She hoped the whole family wasn't going to come pouring in. In her experience relatives always got a shock at the first sight of a body just after death. It wasn't that the dear departed was dead, they looked as if they could never have been alive. She hoped, too, they weren't going to blame Ruth because she hadn't been on the spot at the crucial moment. That was the sort of ill-luck that could occur to anyone. Ruth was a working girl, she couldn't afford to leave with a dubious recommendation.

The feet stopped outside the door and Roger came reluctantly just over the threshold, with his sister and wife behind him. Kate was hesitating in the passage.

'I've rung up Dr Freeman just to acquaint him with the position,' he said rather stiffly. 'I dare say he'll be over in the morning.'

The three came nearer the bed, Roger muttered something about looking very peaceful. Nurse supposed he felt he ought to say that. By tomorrow she'd look much more natural, though all this talk of looking so peaceful and so young was a lot of baloney in Nurse's opinion. All right when the dead person was young, of course . . . It was a relief to her when they all tiptoed out again, as if they were afraid of disturbing her, she whom no one would ever disturb again. It was Dorothy who repeated, 'Where is Mrs Appleyard? I'm going to see.'

11

Nurse saw them all go, with a sense of relief. She had an odd sense of unease, as if something wasn't quite all right. She couldn't think what it was. Something Dorothy had said? She looked round but the room yielded no clue. 'Getting fanciful in my old age,' said Nurse Alexander robustly. She went along the passage to fetch hot water. Queer when you were so well-off to have everything so uncomfortable, but she'd noticed it before with rich people. No conveniences according to present-day standards, no running water . . . 'Running water?' she imagined the old woman saying. 'I don't expect to sleep in a bathroom.' Always had someone to wait on her, of course, that was the fact. She came back with the big enamel jug and the little copper jug and approached the bed. She took the head, lying slightly askew on the pillow, between her hands. Then she saw the mark on the upper lip.

It was nothing much, like a small bruise that had bled a little, only—it hadn't been there when she went along to the bathroom before tea. She was sure of that. Well, she should know, always sponging the poor old thing's face. 'How did you come to do a thing like that?' she wondered. 'Did you come round in that last minute, cry out perhaps, fling up a hand?' Not out of the question but—shocking if it were true. Wisest to sponge the mark away as best you could. Not likely anyone else would notice.

She pulled the shade off the light, and her uneasiness grew. Because there had been a little blood flowing, you could see where it dried, only—she began to feel queer. It wasn't natural. Blood should run down on to the sheet, or trickle on to the chin. It shouldn't dry like—like an envelope over which blotting paper has been pressed. She looked about her. Handkerchief, still tucked under the pillow, and no blood on it anyway. None on the pillow-case, none on the old-fashioned nightie. And then she noticed something else, something so small that in other circumstances it wouldn't even have seemed important. The cushion that she'd left on the little chair beside the bed was now on the big chair by the fireplace.

'Be your age,' she told herself sensibly, 'you threw it back, naturally enough, you just don't remember. People can't recall every single detail.'

But she wasn't reassured. She crossed the room and picked up the cushion, took it over to the light. One of the buttons had a little chip in it—she'd noticed that before today—and just round this button and even on the button itself was a faint discoloration. It wasn't much, if you weren't looking for it you mightn't even notice. Only—she was. She touched it with a speculative finger. Quite fresh, she decided, a light rust-colour, the colour—the colour of dried blood. And then she realised what it was that had nagged at her mind, the thing Dorothy had said that she hadn't been able to nail down—until now. There was no light under the door, she had said. That was what had attracted her attention. But when Nurse left the room the bedside lamp had been on. It was never switched off. And it *had* been off when Nurse came up from downstairs. So that was proof positive that someone had been into the room after she left it.

'Well, but I knew that. It was Ruth Appleyard. I heard the door shut.'

Now she thought it was very strange that Ruth shouldn't have put in an appearance. That must be for one of two reasons. Either because she didn't know anything had happened. Or because she did. 'She can't,' said Nurse robustly. 'Well, then, why isn't she here?' And why should anyone want to turn off the bedside light—unless something was wrong? According to Mrs Dingle it was off when she looked in. The old woman couldn't have switched it off, so much was certain.

'Dr Freeman won't like this,' Nurse muttered. Come to that, she didn't like it herself. If she hadn't happened to notice the mark—but Freeman was no fool. A person who's been smothered—because by this time Nurse was convinced that was the fact—doesn't, to a doctor's eye, look the same as one who's petered out in a heart attack. She'd have to tell him. Well, of course. Pass the buck to him and let him do whatever he thought right. Not that he had any choice, not now *she* knew. No sense wasting time. Nurse opened the door. She could hear Dorothy's voice a little way off. 'Giving Ruth hell, I suppose,' thought Nurse. The poor girl. Struggled on to duty and couldn't stay the course. That must be about the size of it. That Mrs Dingle with her talk of a headache as if it was nothing. Migraines involved collapse. Kate Waring had shown much more sympathy, been the only one who'd asked about Ruth afterwards, but then she, like Ruth, like Nurse herself, had to earn a living.

'The only men in this house are the women,' reflected Nurse, cryptically, stealing down the stairs, like a large well-fed pussy cat, hoping she'd reach the telephone before anyone leaped out to intercept her. As she touched the instrument she heard a door open somewhere upstairs, and she got her connection quickly before anyone could prevent her. 'I knew this was going to be an unlucky job from the start,' she reflected grimly. 'These people who write crime stories as if it was all muffins and the best butter ought to get mixed up in the real thing. That 'ud larn 'em.' Sordid and sickening, that's what murder was. A rather irascible voice at the other end of the line exploded. 'Yes? Who is it?' and she plunged into her amazing revelation.

When she left the death chamber Dorothy marched along the passage and flung open the door of Ruth's room, without even knocking. The place was in darkness. She pressed the switch and light flowed into the room.

From the bed came a protesting sound as Ruth struggled into a sitting position.

'Mrs Appleyard!' Dorothy sounded indignant. 'Have you been here all the afternoon?'

Ruth blinked at her. 'Could you put out the light?' she murmured. It was the first time any of the Dingles had seen her at a disadvantage.

Dorothy crossed the room and drew back the curtains. A little weak daylight was still left outside, insufficient to see by.

'I'm sorry,' said Ruth, regaining control of herself. 'Do you want me?'

'Nurse said you were with my mother-in-law.' The words were an accusation.

Ruth shook her head carefully, as if she thought it might fall off if it were subjected to any but the gentlest treatment.

'I've been asleep. I took a tablet.'

'I know. I hope your head's better.'

'Not much,' confessed Ruth. 'They last at least twelve hours —and that's when I'm lucky. I'm sorry about Nurse. I thought she knew . . .'

'She said she called and you answered.'

'If so it was in my—stupor,' murmured Ruth. 'Oh!'

'Yes?'

'Something did rouse me, I was conscious of a noise. I didn't associate it with Nurse.'

'So you've been here all the afternoon?'

'I'm sorry,' said Ruth again. You could tell she wasn't herself, Dorothy reflected, or she'd never have been so meek. 'Does Nurse want me in Lady Dingle's room at once?'

'No,' said Dorothy cruelly. 'Not today, or any day. You'll be able to go as soon as you like.'

'I don't think I understand,' Ruth sounded as stupid as an owl.

'No? Let me make it quite clear. My mother-in-law is dead. She died quite alone. Naturally we all thought you were with her.'

'Dead? By herself? I do hope . . .'

'Well?'

'I hope she didn't know anything about it, dying, I mean. She used to say she hoped she'd go without realising it—'

'That's something we shall never be sure about,' Dorothy agreed. 'Still, she's been unconscious to all intents and purposes, so far as we know . . .'

'But we don't know much, do we?' Ruth stood up and moved uncertainly towards the dressing-table, recoiling at the figure coming to meet her in the looking-glass. There were black lines under the eyes, the skin had a yellowish tinge. 'I look as though

I've got jaundice,' she muttered. 'Sometimes they do come round at the last minute.'

As she left the bed a small white cloth fell to the carpet. Dorothy pounced on it.

'I thought you said you'd been in your room all the afternoon, Mrs Appleyard.'

'Yes.' Ruth was smoothing back the roughened ends of hair, rubbing a little colour into the ghastly cheeks.

'This is a visitor's towel from the bathroom.'

'Oh?' Ruth's surprise sounded genuine enough. 'I must have brought it along by mistake.'

'By mistake?'

'The room was full of steam and—I suppose someone had just been having a bath. Yes, that was it. It must have been Nurse's call that brought me up from the depths. ('Of all the extravagant phrases,' thought Dorothy scornfully. 'Up from the depths, indeed!') I felt so horribly ill, I thought I would be sick. I waited for the feeling to go off, but it didn't, so presently I struggled along to the bathroom, and—I suppose I mistook it for my handkerchief.'

Dorothy's brows arched above her full brown eyes. 'Rather a large handkerchief, Mrs Appleyard.'

'Have you ever had a migraine?' asked Ruth. 'No? Then I suppose you wouldn't understand. It knocks you half senseless. I was pretty sick, and I grabbed at what I thought was my handkerchief. All I could see was something white, then I staggered back here.' Slowly the eyes moved round the room. 'Lady Dingle's dead. That's what you said?'

'Yes. Oh pray don't disturb yourself now. If you're really feeling so seedy you wouldn't be much use in the sickroom, and, as I told you, there really isn't anything now for you to do.'

She came away on that, just in time to see Nurse come very quietly from the sickroom and walk down the stairs. She was about to speak when she realised the woman was making for the telephone. There was about her movements something so unusually quiet, so nearly furtive, that Dorothy remained where she was, leaning cautiously over the banisters. She heard the receiver removed and then Nurse called the doctor's number.

'Roger's told him already,' reflected Dorothy irritably. 'Really, one would think this was her house.'

She was about to charge down and break up the call when Nurse got her connection.

'Dr Freeman?' She spoke quietly but to the woman, listening avidly from the floor above, the words were clearly audible. 'I thought I ought to tell you I'm not altogether satisfied that Lady Dingle's death is a natural one. What? Just what I say. I'd like you to see her before I lay her out. Could you . . .? Thank you, Doctor.'

The receiver was gently replaced, and Nurse came padding back. Dorothy just had time to whisk into the gaunt spare room before she came round the bend of the staircase.

When the sickroom door had closed once again Dorothy ran down the stairs to the library, where Roger sat, his head buried in his hands.

'Roger! Something's wrong. She didn't tell you?'

'She?'

'Nurse Alexander. She's just rung Dr Freeman to say she isn't satisfied about your mother's death.'

Roger stared at her, horror-struck. 'What are you talking about, Dot?'

'I told you—she says it's not natural. That means—it means—'

'Nonsense,' said Roger, roughly. 'Of course it's natural. For goodness' sake, Dorothy, don't start a panic in the household.'

'Then why did Nurse Alexander . . .?'

'A bit upset because she wasn't there when it happened. And wants to guard against gossip in the future.'

'What gossip?'

'How on earth do I know? But I dare say it wouldn't do her any special good if it came out that she was guzzling tea while her patient choked herself to death—if that's what happened. Now calm down. Freeman's no fool, he won't want trouble. Where is everyone?'

'I think Isobel's in the kitchen with Kate. No one,' she added irrelevantly, 'would believe she was forty and the mother of two children. She runs up and down like a girl. Mrs Appleyard's still more or less prostrate in her room. I don't know where Frank is; also with Kate, I should think. They seem more or less inseparable.'

'I must let Cecil know,' said Roger, restlessly. He picked up the telephone.

Violet answered the call.

'Is Cecil there? This is Roger speaking.'

'He's just having his tea.'

'Call him please. This is urgent.' His fingers played a restless tattoo on the table-top as he waited.

Cecil said he'd come over at once. 'Roger's playing cautious,' he told Violet. 'There's something not altogether straightforward. I don't like this.' He sounded so troubled that she flung her arms about his neck crying, 'Oh, how typical of her to make trouble for us even after she's dead. Don't look so shocked, darling, you know there was never any love lost between us. Do you think I don't know how you lie awake at night, worrying because you can't see your way clear and she won't help you? Of course I'm not going to shed any tears because it's all over. You shouldn't either. You should be glad, for her sake as much as anyone else's.'

'I don't think it's going to be as simple as that,' murmured Cecil. 'I must go now, I won't be away longer than I can help. Oh, darling, what a family you've married into.'

'I'm not made of sugar,' was Violet's sturdy reply. 'Now, don't let them keep you there all night. You've got me and Junior to think of now, and we need you.'

But though she saw him off comfortingly, smiling and waving, the smile died as she closed the door.

'Not quite straightforward,' she repeated. 'What does that mean? Well, if someone has put a dollop of poison in the old witch's tea, good luck to them, I say, the very best of luck.'

Ruth waited till Dorothy had gone downstairs and then made her way to Lady Dingle's room. Nurse met her on the threshold.

'Well, you look like twopenn'orth of cat's-meat,' she observed, frankly. 'What happened?'

Ruth explained.

'You mean you *didn't* come in?' exclaimed Nurse. 'But someone did because I heard the door shut.'

'Mightn't that have been the wind?'

'It wasn't the wind that put out the light or was responsible for the old lady snuffing it just when she did. I suppose you don't walk in your sleep?'

'No.'

'Well, you may as well get back to bed. I'm waiting for Dr Freeman and he won't want a second patient on his hands. It looks to me,' she added grimly, 'as if we're all going to need our wits about us from now on.'

As Ruth went back to her room the thunder came streaming through the sky like the sound of a diabolical drum.

It was Roger, watching from the morning-room window, who saw Dr Freeman's car stop at the gate, and went out to let him in.

His apologies for bringing the man out were brusquely cut short. 'Nonsense,' said the doctor, 'that's my job.' He went upstairs without another word.

Nurse told her story, but it didn't take that to make him realise this wasn't a natural death. He carried the cushion over to the light and stood there with it in his hands for some minutes. Nurse didn't dare speak or move. At last he said, 'This is going to be uncommonly awkward. I wouldn't have had this happen for a thousand pounds. I've known the Dingles all my life . . . Yes, yes, Nurse, of course you were right to ring me. You hadn't any choice, though whoever is responsible for this must have banked on my sending over the certificate without coming up again.'

'What are you going to do?' asked Nurse.

'Do? I haven't any choice either. I shall tell the coroner I'm not satisfied. After that, the matter's out of my hands. Those wretched sons! They've had trouble enough without this—the old man should have been certified, leaving such a will.'

He seemed suddenly aware of Nurse's eyes, fixed in fascination on his face.

'Don't pay any attention to what I say, Nurse. I'm getting to be an old man. I talk to myself. One of these days I dare say someone 'ull suggest it's time I was put away.'

When the family realised that Dr Freeman wasn't going to sign the certificate they were shocked beyond measure.

'What did you expect?' demanded Freeman. 'That I should connive at a crime? That's what I said, a crime. Try and get it into your heads that this isn't a natural death. To put it more bluntly, I believe your mother was murdered.'

They sat together in the library, Roger, Dorothy, Cecil, Isobel. 'Murder!' they said under their breaths, finding it of a sudden uncommonly hard to meet each other's eyes. Because, though Freeman was getting on, he was no fool. If he said it was murder the odds were he was right.

'But how?' persisted Dorothy.

'He didn't say.'

'Where's Nurse?'

'With *her*. Freeman said he thought the rest of us should keep out of the room for the present. Nurse has the key.'

'That woman!' breathed Dorothy.

'It's sensible enough,' Cecil muttered. 'At least she had no motive. Mamma was nothing but a job to her. Now she's out of work. Who else was there this afternoon?'

'If we knew that,' said Roger, 'the problem would be solved.'

Their eyes slewed round, each waiting for the other to speak. 'I don't think it's any good our jumping to conclusions,' Isobel said at last. 'The matter's out of our hands now.'

'There is one thing,' said Dorothy slowly. 'It may be just coincidence, of course.'

'Isobel's right,' broke in Cecil, hurriedly. 'It's best to wait.'

'I was wondering if I should say anything.'

'What is it?' snapped Roger, whose nerves were at breaking-point.'

'I went into the room a few days ago and Mrs Appleyard was standing by the bed with that cushion in her hands bending over Mamma. As soon as she saw me she dropped it. She said she was conducting an experiment.'

'What experiment?'

'She didn't tell me.'

'We don't know that the cushion had anything to do with it,' said Isobel.

'No,' agreed Dorothy quickly, 'of course not. Only—it wasn't anything obvious because we saw her—your mother, I mean —we didn't notice . . . It was only when Nurse started to prepare the body . . . No—blood . . .' Her voice trailed away.

They were still conjecturing—Who? Why? How?—with long pauses between their speeches when the police arrived.

12

The case was in the hands of Inspector Moss, with a local sergeant named Bryce as his assistant. While they waited for Holles's arrival—the lawyer had named four o'clock as the probable time—he went over the various statements he had taken from members of the household.

'There are some unusual factors here,' he observed. 'As a rule amateur criminals, particularly in murder cases, give themselves away by producing a detailed statement to account for every possible minute of their time, and fake an alibi if they haven't got a genuine one. But all the people here might be experts. Each of them has given a collection of facts, of which very few can be proved—and they don't seem to care. Here's the truth, they say, do what you like with it. That makes it hard for us. If they give us false evidence we've only got to discover where they made their mistake. It's when they don't offer any proof of their evidence that we're likely to be dished. I wasn't there, I don't know, I don't remember. What on earth can you do with that?

'There's no doubt about the cause of death, but whoever's responsible has the wit to realise that that cushion doesn't give us any lead at all. A child could have used it with effect, seeing the old lady's condition. We can't hope to prove anything by fingerprints. Admittedly half the household were in the sickroom that day, and most of them after death. And they've all got good reasons for being there. Nurse Alexander, Mrs Appleyard (she helped in the morning), both the Dingles, Mrs Exeter, Miss Waring (she took nurse up a cup of coffee at eleven o'clock)—the only two people who say they didn't go in were Cecil Dingle and young Hardy. Now take the individual statements. Start with Roger Dingle.

'Roger said:
I went into the library after lunch to write letters. My wife was with me for a short time but soon left me to attend to some concerns of her own. No, I don't know what they were, she didn't tell me and I didn't ask. It wouldn't occur to me to do so. I didn't telephone and there were no incoming calls. I wasn't interrupted until about half-past three when my brother, Cecil, arrived. I saw him from the window and let him in. He stayed about a quarter of an hour. He didn't go upstairs. I saw him off at about a quarter to four. A little later my sister, Mrs Exeter, came in and we were together until my wife arrived with the staggering news of my mother's death. I believe I visited the downstairs cloak-room after seeing my brother off. I didn't see anyone going or coming. I didn't hear any voices or sounds of any kind.

'Nothing much to help us there,' was Moss's comment. 'We know his brother left about a quarter to four, because the nurse confirms it. She heard their voices from the floor above. We know, from Mrs Exeter's evidence and Mr Hardy's, that he met them at the gate, and stayed talking to Mrs Exeter for a few minutes before he went off in his car. He says he didn't see anyone else or hear any particular sounds in the house. If the other two are speaking the truth, it doesn't seem as though Cecil Dingle can be involved.

'The same goes for Mrs Exeter. She corroborates the stories we already know, and Mrs Dingle agrees that she was in the library when she (Mrs D.) broke in with her news.

'Mrs Dingle's more hopeful from a policeman's point of view. Here's her evidence, with nothing to back it up. She says:

After leaving my husband soon after lunch I went up to the attics to look for a big silver buckle that I wanted for my new dress. I knew my mother-in-law hadn't set eyes on it for years, but she was rather possessive and didn't like parting with things, even if she was never going to use them again. I don't remember seeing anyone on my way upstairs. Nurse Alexander was with my mother-in-law and I remember Mrs Appleyard saying she had a headache and was going to lie down. I didn't realise it was serious enough to incapacitate her, or I would have arranged to take over from Nurse when she went to her tea. I didn't find the buckle I was looking for, the attics are like a jungle, you pick your way over old gladstone bags and picture frames with broken glasses and rolls of ancient linoleum and picnic baskets and cardboard boxes filled with scraps. I came upon a photograph album about twenty years old and I became engrossed in it. I realised presently it was getting dark and must be time for tea, so I came down and went into my room to get tidy. There was no light on the lower landing—I have since been told the bulb flickered out during the afternoon and I noticed there was no light on in my mother-in-law's room. You can see a gold bar under the door even when only the bed-side lamp is on. I opened the door and found the room quite dark except for the fire. I put on the central light and went over to the bed. I saw at once there had been a great change and went down to look for Nurse. She was having tea in the kitchen and said quite confidently that Mrs Appleyard was in the sickroom. I don't remember whether she said she had actually seen her go in, but she was quite sure she was there. After I had told my husband I went up to Mrs Appleyard's room. She was lying on the bed in the dark, and said she had not left the room since lunch. Later she agreed she had gone along to the bathroom. It was not seeing any light under the door of Lady Dingle's room that made me go in.'

'That's a rum story, sir,' offered Bryce. 'Why choose a cold winter's afternoon to go up to the attics—there's no central heating in that house—to look for a buckle she hadn't seen for years and couldn't even be sure was up there? It's not as if she had to have it in a tearing hurry, they weren't going to a party or anything.'

'On the other hand, Bryce, they most likely were going back to London very shortly. They were expecting this chap, Holles, the next day. After he came it mightn't be so easy to help herself to any little picking she fancied. Then she'd nothing special to do—and women are inclined to act on impulse. No, it doesn't sound an impossible story, but it would be better for her if she'd mentioned to her husband what she'd intended to do, or if anyone had seen her go up the attic stairs. You see, we've only her word for it that the light was out when she came down. It makes a fine excuse for her to go into a room I gather she visited as seldom as possible. *There was no light, I thought that odd, I went in.*'

'You mean, the light may have been on, she peeped in—nothing strange about that, the old lady was her husband's mother—she found the room empty, the cushion was there, what a chance—as you say, women are creatures of impulse. Then—come down and give the alarm. What about motive, sir?'

'Whoever is responsible the motive is obvious—money. Both the Dingle sons were up a gum-tree, financially, both had been hoping to make a touch. The old lady had never executed any power of attorney; if they wanted the money in a hurry it might have been awkward. Both stood to gain under this new will no one has seen, but that the old lady outlined to them on the last day she was capable of talking sense to anyone. Roger Dingle's given me the figures. He gets £5,000, his brother gets £1,000. Each grandchild gets £5,000 but the only grandchildren to date are the Exeter boys. As far as money goes, Mrs Exeter has the greatest motive, but it's hard to see how she could have gone into the room and no proof whatever that she and her husband needed the money. Cecil Dingle would have profited by his mother remaining alive till after his child is born in April and he, too, seems to lack opportunity.

'Now for the other two women on the premises. Take Miss Waring's statement. Kate said:

I was in the kitchen most of the afternoon, preparing things for dinner. A little before four I put on the kettle for tea. I generally make tea for Nurse and myself at four o'clock and take the family their tea about four-thirty. I wasn't upstairs after half-past three and didn't hear any sounds that attracted my attention. I remember that Nurse came down a little later than usual. She said Mrs Appleyard was with Lady Dingle. No, I don't remember if she said she had seen or only heard her. I didn't know Cecil Dingle had called till Mr Hardy mentioned it. It was about 4.30 when Mrs Dingle came to summon Nurse.

'And she knew Mrs A. had this migraine and was lying down,' added Moss. 'She wasn't sure if she'd be fit to carry on, but was reassured by Nurse. Now we come to Mrs Appleyard herself. All she says is she never left her room that afternoon except to go to the bathroom. It must have been four or a little after because the atmosphere was still steamy. She agrees she didn't speak of the visit till after Mrs Dingle challenged her, she says she didn't think it was important as she hadn't been near the old lady's room.

'Well, that's the lot except Frank Hardy, who I think can be counted out. He says simply he came back with Mrs Exeter, went along to the billiard-room and knocked up the balls till about half-past four. He didn't see anyone, except Cecil Dingle on his way in, and nobody seemed to be moving about. He had half an hour to spare—it all sounds reasonable enough.'

'They all sound reasonable, except perhaps Mrs Dingle,' Bryce volunteered.

'That shows you that X. isn't a fool. Now let's examine the motives. Roger Dingle needed money and needed it quickly. A mortgage was falling in and he couldn't meet it. He was badly in debt and his bank wouldn't help. He admits he's got a heavy overdraft and no immediate prospects. He couldn't offer his mother as security without her consent, and the old lady's reputation seems to be fairly well known. She had the complete control of her money, she might leave Roger £25,000 on Tuesday and the same number of pence next week. No sane man's going to take that sort of bet. It's possible Roger *could* have gone up after his brother went. Mrs Exeter and Mr Hardy weren't expected back till later—that came out while we were talking—Miss Waring would be in the kitchen—there was only Mrs Appleyard and she had this migraine. Mrs Roger affects to believe it was just a headache that would go off in an hour or so. But Miss Waring knew that migraines can't be so lightly discounted and there's no reason to suppose Roger didn't know the same. The room would be empty—if it hadn't been, he could simply have said he was passing and looked in to see how his mother was—it wouldn't take long to put a cushion over the old woman's face . . . Of course, if he did it, he took chances. He might have been seen coming down, but he could have said he'd gone to his bedroom to fetch a handkerchief or something . . . I'm inclined to think, Bryce, that the timing was deliberate. Once Holles was here everyone's hands would have been tied. For one thing, there'd have been one more possible witness, and that an impartial one. Well, there's the case against Roger Dingle. We've debated Mrs Roger. For my part, I think Mrs Exeter and Cecil Dingle are both out for the same reason, that they simply didn't have the opportunity. That leaves Miss Waring and Mrs Appleyard. Miss Waring says she was in the kitchen. She can't offer any more proof than anyone else, but under the new will she only gets £500 which isn't a fortune. On the other hand, this house has been her home for thirty years. Lady Dingle's death simply means she's out of a job at an age when it's not easy for women to find fresh employment, particularly when they've been in one job so long. They get into certain ways, find it difficult to adapt themselves. No, I can't see she had much motive for murdering the old woman. Then—Mrs Appleyard. She comes into a large legacy if the old woman dies before Mrs A gets her discharge. The sons say they would have contested the will—at least Roger does—but hanging your family washing on the line doesn't do a barrister any good. His record is that he's industrious and honest, but never quite manages to hit the jackpot. On the face of it, Mrs Appleyard is our most likely suspect. She stood to get a large sum of money, provided Lady Dingle died within, say, forty-eight hours. She says she didn't go near the room, but we know she left her own at about the time the old woman must have been smothered. No one actually saw her enter, but Nurse says her door was open when she (Nurse) went into the bathroom to turn on the bath water, and closed a few minutes later. She had no means, no relatives and, I should say, a hell of a lot of ambition. Yes, so far as motive and opportunity are concerned, I should say she tops the list.'

'Quite so,' agreed Bryce, 'but—anyone else in the household could recognise that as easily as you or me. Suppose murder was planned, then the obvious thing would be to bring it off before Mrs Appleyard left the house. X. would know you can't prove you were lying down with a migraine right through the afternoon. It's a question of one person's word against another—and, as you say, her motive is glaring.'

'Been reading some of these whodunits, Bryce?' asked the inspector in a dry voice. 'I've ploughed through some myself and I realise that in them the crime's usually committed by the least probable person, but in real life it's the other way about. It's the husband kills the wife, not some mysterious lover, the wife who poisons her husband, not some confederate he met in Cuba in the year dot. The most obvious suspect here is Mrs Appleyard. I don't say she did it, but that fact doesn't automatically prove her innocence. The quickest way to a given point is always a straight line, Bryce, my lad, and don't you forget it.'

'Ruth,' said Frank Hardy, abruptly, 'have you got a lawyer?'

'Only Mr Devenish and he's in a nursing-home. Why? Are you thinking about Roger's threat to contest the will?'

'No,' said Frank in the same tone, 'but I think in your own interest you ought to be represented at the inquest. Holles is coming down today, isn't he? He'll act for the Dingles.'

'I don't need anyone.'

'Oh Ruth, don't be absurd. Of course you do. There's a chap I know in London, a queer fish, a sort of rogue elephant in the profession—'

'So you think he's particularly suited to me?'

'His motto is my clients are always innocent. That's why, if he'll take it on, you must have him.'

'Must? You mean, you think the Dingles are going to try and push this on to *me*?'

He said, 'I'm your friend, Ruth, probably the only one you've got in this household. And you're going to need all the help you can get. You see, I *know* you were in Lady Dingle's room that afternoon. I saw you go in.'

There was a moment of complete silence. Then Ruth said

evenly, 'That's nonsense. I wasn't near her yesterday afternoon.'

'Oh Ruth, do be reasonable. I tell you I saw you. I saw you come out of your room and go into hers.'

'I went to the bathroom. It was full of steam.'

'That was afterwards. Before that you were in Lady Dingle's room.'

'Where were you?' asked Ruth.

'I was coming up the back stairs. I'd left Isobel talking to her brother. And—*I saw you, Ruth.*'

'You didn't tell the police that?'

'No.'

'Won't they think that strange? Perjury's a crime, isn't it?'

'I didn't commit perjury. I didn't tell them anything that wasn't true.'

'I wonder if they'd agree. It's casuistry at best. Why are you telling me now?'

'You must be on your guard.'

'In case you change your mind?'

'The police aren't fools.'

'You mean they may worm it out of you?'

'I mean, you must be represented. And Crook's your best man if you can get him.'

'Because he'd wink at a little murder?'

'I didn't say that. You could have gone along to take over, couldn't you, and then felt too faint and gone back? There are only two explanations in a case like this. You did it—or you didn't. Crook will stand for it that you didn't. You don't have to prove innocence.'

'And the accused gets the benefit of the doubt. I know all about that. I've been there before. But there's one thing you're overlooking, Frank.'

'What's that?'

'*You* haven't any proof either.'

'You mean, I might have invented the whole thing?' He sounded amazed. 'Why should I?'

'I'm sure your Mr Crook could find an answer to that. There's one infallible reason why people suppress evidence.'

'You tell me,' Frank invited her.

'Because it's worth their while.'

'But you—' He stopped. 'Ruth, you can't mean—'

'No? Frank, listen. We've got the gloves off with a vengeance now. Under Lady Dingle's will, I inherit £10,000—'

'Assuming you're not found guilty of her death.'

'I shan't be. I wasn't in the room. The only other person, according to yourself, who could give any evidence against me, is you. You say you saw me, but you didn't tell the police. It might be suggested you'd got your reasons.'

'I see,' said Frank slowly with a sort of unemphatic disgust. 'So that's what you think of me—a blackmailer.'

'And you think of me as a murderess. There's not much to choose between us, is there?'

'There are times,' said Frank, in a savage voice, 'when I could strangle you—with pleasure.'

'So on the whole,' concluded Ruth, paying no attention to the last remark, 'I don't think I'll bother your wonderful Mr Crook.'

'Perhaps later you'll change your mind.'

'It'll all depend—on which of us the police believe. If they fall for your story that'll be the day to call in your wonder-man and watch him do his stuff.'

13

Shortly after four o'clock Mr Rupert Holles drove up in the station taxi and caused an instant flutter in the dovecotes by saying flatly he'd never seen the will since he sent the draft to Lady Dingle. For all he knew, it hadn't been executed and wasn't worth the paper it was written on. At this information Roger's eyes bulged, Dorothy threw up her head apprehensively, Kate said, 'But it came, I remember that. I took it in myself, a registered envelope. Ruth! Did you post it back?'

'No,' said Ruth calmly. 'I only saw it once. That must have been the—the 23rd, it was the day before the visitors started arriving. Lady Dingle was sitting at that black oak desk in her bedroom where she kept all her private papers, reading something that I'm sure was a will.'

'Did you see her sign it?'

'There wasn't time. I was only in the room about a minute. I'd come up to ask her something and when I got the answer I went away.'

'Then presumably it's among her papers. I don't know how much licence the police-inspector has taken with her belongings.' He went off, a little pompous, impressive figure, to show the law he wasn't to be put upon.

'I can scarcely believe it,' murmured Cecil. 'You mean, it's been in the house all this time. I suppose it's in her black desk.'

'No,' said Dorothy, in a voice of such controlled violence that they all turned to stare.

'How can you be sure?'

'Because I looked—one day when I was sitting with her.'

'But she keeps the desk locked.'

'I know. But I knew where she kept the key. In her purse. It was really seeing the purse lying on the side that gave me the idea. You see, I couldn't quite believe that she, even she, could draw up such a—malicious—will as the one she'd described to us. You know how she loved to play tricks on us, keep us on tenterhooks, always, always, reminding us that the money was hers. Well, the thought suddenly came into my head— Perhaps this is another of your diabolical tricks. And there was the key. And no one likely to interrupt me for an hour anyway. I felt, as Mrs Gusset says, as though it were meant.'

Roger's eyes, pale, opaque, were fixed on hers. They didn't waver.

'So you opened the drawer and . . .'

'It wasn't there. I looked everywhere. So naturally I supposed she'd sent it back to Mr Holles.'

'I suppose you realise the construction that may be put on your crazy action, Dorothy.'

Dorothy started. 'I don't understand.'

'Don't you? Think for a moment—imagine if Kate—or Cecil had opened the drawer, two people who suffer under the new will . . .'

'You mean they may think I destroyed it? Well, I didn't, because it wasn't there. But if I had I consider I should have been justified. No one could blame me.'

'I really think, Dorothy, you've taken leave of your senses.' Roger sounded horrified. 'Of course everyone would blame you. It's a criminal act . . .'

'Well, I didn't find it because it wasn't there, so I couldn't destroy it. Mr Holles *must* have it unless—unless she'd destroyed it herself. She's quite capable—was quite capable—of playing the cruellest tricks on us.'

'Kate, don't you know whether it was posted?' Roger appeared to dismiss the subject so far as his wife was concerned.

'I didn't post it, if that's what you mean,' replied Kate. 'I never actually saw it.'

'But you knew it had come?'

'I told you—I took in a long legal-looking envelope on the morning of the—the 23rd I think it would be. It was registered and I took it for granted it was a new will. Mr Holles had been down for lunch quite recently and when he went he said to your mother, rather stiffly, as if he didn't really approve, "Then, Lady Dingle, I will carry out your instructions without delay."

I remember her saying with a sort of chuckle, "That's right. At my age, time and tide are both on the ebb." Afterwards, I remember thinking how prophetic the words were. I gave the envelope to your mother, who took it without any comment and that's the last I ever saw of it.'

'Did she happen to speak of it, to say it was posted, to . . .?'

'Not to me. You might ask Ruth. She was very much more your mother's confidante during these last months.'

But Ruth said no, she hadn't posted it. The afternoon of the 23rd had turned out dull and rainy, and neither she nor Lady Dingle had been out. The following day the family started to arrive and Lady Dingle hadn't been out that day either. Perhaps Kate . . .?

But Roger said no, Kate hadn't been asked to post it either.

Mr Holles came back, looking somewhat deflated. He wanted to know if anyone had actually seen the will witnessed.

'I take it we're all beneficiaries,' said Roger.

Mr Holles glared. 'I had appreciated that. But there are servants—and visitors—what about the doctor?'

'It can't have been the doctor,' said Kate, 'because he didn't come to the house after it arrived, until we sent for him early on Christmas morning.'

Mrs Gusset said you wouldn't catch her putting her name in writing without knowing what it was all about. Mrs Gamp wasn't in the family's employ any more, but she was wanting, anyhow, so it would be a waste of time asking her. Besides, there had to be two.

'Well, then,' said Dorothy, 'probably it never was witnessed. It was all a cruel joke on her part. She destroyed it . . .'

Ruth said suddenly, 'Sealing-wax. She asked for sealing-wax. She wasn't sending any registered packets and she never sealed her letters. But she might have fastened up the will and sealed it.'

'Why seal it unless you mean to post it?'

Ruth's silence was eloquent and Holles hurriedly passed on to the next point.

'Are you sure no one came to see her?'

The words were scarcely out of his mouth before Ruth exclaimed, 'Of course. Why didn't we think of it? The two women from the Self-Help Association. They came selling baby clothes. Lady Dingle saw them. Kate (Kate had just joined them), didn't you say they came every year and this was the first time they'd been allowed over the threshold?'

'Yes, that's true, of course. I did wonder . . .'

'And she asked me particularly how many there were . . . Oh, and something else. Kate, do you remember when you were putting down one of the little matinee jackets Lady Dingle said, "Take care, there's a blob of ink—get some blotting paper." But she'd paid for the things in cash—there was some debate about the change—so why should anyone use a pen, unless . . .?'

'This is all speculation,' broke in Holles. 'However, it's easily susceptible of proof. Where do these people live?'

'The office address is in Malcolm Street,' said Kate. 'I don't know where these two lived. One of them was named Mrs Archer—the other one called her that. The office would know.'

She clenched her hands in sudden anger. 'We might have realised no one ever got the better of your mother.'

'It's on the cards that Lady Dingle entrusted the signed document to one of these ladies to post,' said Mr Holles in his pompous way.

'If so,' asked Ruth simply, 'where is it now?'

No one found any answer to that.

Mrs Archer and Miss Trott were sisters, who, after a widely different experience of life, Dolly Archer having covered half the world with a globe-trotting husband while her sister worked for her living in a cathedral town, now found themselves in a similar situation. Their differences of temperament and experience made them excellent company for each other and, since they seldom agreed on anything, their life was never dull. The arrival of a policeman, although in plain clothes, was the highlight of Miss Trott's week. She said that dear Dolly hadn't had her advantage of never dealing with any but an incorruptible police force. The police were the friends of all righteous citizens. (Crook, when he heard this, said indulgently, 'If people like to kid themselves, what's the harm?') Both sisters agreed that they had been asked to witness the late Lady Dingle's will, and had accepted her very reasonable explanation that she couldn't expect any member of her household to oblige her because they were all mentioned in it.

'There's a great deal to be said for the old ways,' sighed Mrs Archer, envisioning a long list of faithful retainers shortly to become pensioners.

'I dare say they've earned it,' was Miss Trott's more acid comment.

But when Moss went on to inquire if they had been asked to post the document, they both shook their heads. Mrs Archer got in first with the information that the old lady had remarked she didn't trust the posts at Christmas time and she intended to keep the will beside her until deliveries were more normal.

'So sad for her not living to see her grandchild,' cooed Mrs Archer.

'She looked to me the sort of grandmother Red Riding Hood found when she reached the cottage in the woods,' was Miss Trott's pithy comment.

Moss, having learned what he came for, took his leave. The sisters had a delightful morning speculating on the reason for his visit.

'She's hidden the will where no one can find it,' breathed Mrs Archer, visualising secret panels in the wall.

'More likely someone got at it and burnt it,' retorted Miss Trott, always more realistic in her attitude towards life.

The situation at Dingle Hall was now very tricky indeed. The most meticulous search failed to reveal a sign of a will. Members of the household began to give Dorothy what are known as old-fashioned looks. Holles, who had been told by the conscientious Roger of his wife's action, gave the impression that in his opinion any further search would be a waste of time.

Holles had supplied Moss with the details of the previous will that would now come into force, unless evidence was obtained of the deliberate destruction of the last will by someone other than the testator and without her concurrence. In that case, steps would be taken to give effect to the dead woman's intentions. Holles had his notes and a copy of the draft will, and there was proof that this will had, in fact, been executed.

'But no proof,' he reminded Moss, sternly, 'that Lady Dingle did not herself destroy it later. You don't know her as I did; she might very well have gone to all this trouble and expense merely to discover the reactions of her relatives.'

'I thought you said there was no question of her being *non compos mentis*,' was Moss's blunt retort, to which Holles replied that no such suggestion had ever been made, and if people were going to be certified because they behaved in unreasonable ways the Commissioners for Lunacy would find themselves working overtime.

The legacies, that had been revoked by the vanished will, were as follows:

To Roger Dingle—£10,000 and the remainder of the estate in goods and money when other legacies, death duties, etc., had been settled.

To Cecil Dingle—£7,500.

To Isobel Exeter—£5,000 plus legacies of £2,000 each to her two children.

To Kate Waring—£100 for every completed year of service, and the remainder to Roger.

'So Kate Waring gets roughly £3,000 and Roger Dingle's share would be about £16,000 when death duties were paid. Did Lady Dingle's family know of these provisions?' asked Moss.

Holles said he understood they did.

'So Roger, Cecil Dingle and Miss Waring lose considerably by the new will. Mrs Exeter and Mrs Appleyard, whose name doesn't, of course, appear in the 1952 will, both gain. According to Mrs Dingle, the will had disappeared from the drawer, assuming that it was kept there, before Mrs Exeter reached the house. If Lady Dingle lived until, say, the end of April, Cecil Dingle's position would improve, provided the infant survived. His share would then be £6,000, but even at that less than under the previous will. Every member of the household could presumably have found occasion to destroy the document, though the brothers seldom spent much time in the sick-room. Still, for an affair like this, very little time would be required. Mrs Dingle and Miss Waring undertook to share with the nursing—well, the watching, really—and Mrs Appleyard also. It could scarcely be in Mrs Appleyard's interest for the will to be destroyed.'

This might be true, but it was equally certain that it had been extremely convenient for Ruth that Lady Dingle should have died precisely when she did. Under questioning, she said frankly that she had had no reason to suppose the will had been destroyed at that time though now she had no doubt . . .

Moss stopped her. 'You have no definite information that the will is no longer in existence? Then your opinions, Mrs Apple-yard, do not constitute evidence.'

'All the same,' persisted Ruth, 'it must be clear that who-ever did destroy the will intended to—defraud me.'

'It is possible that the intent was to safeguard a personal provision,' Moss pointed out in his stiffest manner. 'If and when proof of wilful destruction by another party is forthcoming the provisions of the last will can be implemented in law. But there is at present no proof that Lady Dingle didn't destroy the will herself.'

'But when? She told the family that night—she had no oppor-tunity thereafter . . .'

'There is no proof the will was actually in existence when she told them. And—surely she came up to her room between tea-time and dinner? That would have been an opportunity . . .'

'I helped her to dress,' said Ruth, shortly. 'Besides, what about her last words to me that night? "Don't let them drive you away," she said. "Promise you'll stay with me." There's one thing, the family believed the will was in existence—at all events Roger Dingle did, or he wouldn't have been so anxious to get me off the premises. Well, what happens now?'

'That,' said Moss in grim tones, 'will rest with the coroner's jury.'

A coroner's jury of seven men found Ruth Appleyard guilty of the wilful murder of Emily Dingle and she was formally arrested the same day. The next morning she was brought before a magistrate and was committed for trial at the next Sessions.

Arthur Crook, along with about two million others in London, read the verdict in the evening papers. His first thought was for the young man he'd met at the Blue Bottle.

'Wonder if he had the sense to take my advice,' he reflected. 'I ought to have charged him six-and-eightpence. Then he might have considered it seriously. Chaps never value anything they get for nothing.'

14

Crook was hard at it in his eyrie in Brandon Street when he heard steps on the stairs and knew that the visitor must be seeking him, since no one else lived on the top floor. He came charging out on to the landing, as new as ninepence despite the hour, and found himself looking down on the fair-crested head of the young man, Frank Hardy.

'Pub out of beer?' he enquired genially. 'Well you've come to the right place. My stock came in this morning.'

His room was square, unimaginative and, to a casual visitor, unspeakably dreary. Papers littered the table and the air was cloudy with the horrid little cigars Crook smoked after working hours. He opened a cupboard and produced a large dark bottle and two glasses.

'Having a little trouble?' he asked in the same cheerful voice, pouring out the beer.

'It's Ruth Appleyard,' said Frank.

'How that girl does crop up.' Crook passed a glass across the table.

'They've arrested her for the murder of Lady Dingle. She's so damned pig-headed, she wouldn't take my advice.'

'Don't let that worry you,' said Crook. 'Dames hardly ever do and it's generally just as well. Because when things go wrong you'll find it's always your fault for telling them.'

'I wanted her to get you to represent her at the inquest, but she wouldn't. She said she didn't need a lawyer.'

'Well, she knows better now. Let's have one thing clear at the start. Did she do it?'

'I don't know,' said Frank woodenly. 'I only know she could have done. She was there, she can't prove she didn't go into the room, it was immensely to her advantage . . .'

'I've read the case, too,' said Crook, patiently. 'I mean,

anything to tell me that hasn't got into the press?'

'No,' said Frank in the same wooden voice. 'Nothing.'

'I see,' said Crook. 'What am I supposed to do?'

'I'm here to ask you to take on the defence. Her own lawyer's in hospital, she doesn't seem to know anyone else, she doesn't even seem to appreciate her danger. She just says over and over, "They can't prove I did it. No one will ever be able to prove it." '

'H'm.' Crook refilled their glasses. 'She knows how much that's worth. She's had one Not Proven verdict already.'

'I know. That's why she needs all the help she can get. Will you take it on? I know it's a risk . . .'

'Some risks I don't mind taking,' Crook pointed out. 'I don't mind riskin' not gettin' my bill paid, because if X. don't pay me Y. does. I see to that. And I don't mind riskin' my life, because I do that every time I cross the road. But the one thing I can't afford to gamble with is my reputation. You'll find chaps whose names are written in the Law List in letters of gold who'll tell you a corkscrew's one half of a pair of parallel lines compared with me. You don't have to believe them. But I can't afford to act for someone who's going to be found guilty. And, on the face of it, it looks to me remarkably likely Mrs Apple-yard is going to find herself for the high jump.'

'Not if you act for her. She hasn't got anyone unless you count me—and Nurse Alexander.'

'Oh, she thinks she's innocent, does she?'

'To tell you the truth, I don't think she cares.'

'Another person without a conscience. What's she like?'

'One of these big jolly women. Cut you in half with a saw as soon as look at you. All in a day's work. Boasts she was once followed from Liverpool to London on account of her figure, but it must have been a long time ago. Figures like that went out with Edward VII.'

'More's the pity,' said Crook. 'I never fancied these anchovy-fork types myself. Middle-aged, I take it?'

'Don't they say you can tell a woman's age by the songs she sings? Well, she was roaring The Only Girl In The World fit to beat the band that night. Lucky in a way you can't hear in the front of the house. Roger Dingle has feudal ideas about that sort of thing, according to Kate Waring. Well, that dates her, doesn't it?'

'Dates me, too,' said Crook. 'I must have sung that song all over London and Gay Paree in my time. P'raps Nursie was thinking of her great romance . . .'

'The chap who followed her from Liverpool? I couldn't help feeling a pang of sympathy for the Only Boy in the World. She sounded as if she was lying in wait for him with a meat axe.'

'I believe there are tribes that consider that a show of affection. By the way, how about declaring an interest yourself? A case of Little Dan Cupid?'

'She wouldn't look at me,' said Frank hastily.

'You're a young man,' offered Crook, kindly, sounding like Cinderella's Fairy Godmother. 'It's when women don't look at you you want to start running. Remember those beasts in the Revelations who had eyes before and behind? Well, I wouldn't mind betting a pony all those beasts were females.'

But though eventually he agreed to undertake the case (his heel of Achilles being an inability to pass up a chance of wiping the official eye), he found the wheel of his aged yellow Rolls (that had replaced the famous little red Scourge) turning to a perpetual chant, over and over.

'What if she did?' they rumbled, 'what if she did?'

When Crook came lumbering into Ruth's cell he was greeted with a stare of such amazement that he came to a dead stop.

'Take it easy, sugar,' he said encouragingly, 'it often takes them this way at the first time of meeting, but they get over it.'

'Mr Crook?' said Ruth. If he had expected to find her overwhelmed by this fresh disaster he was pleasantly surprised. She held her head high and her manner was spirited and defiant.

'The one and only. Now, sugar, you and me are going to have a conference. What you have to remember is I'm absolutely dependent on you. I can make bricks with the smallest amount of straw known to mortal man, but—' he spread his big hands—'no straw, no bricks.'

'I can't change my story now,' said Ruth, in her deep voice. 'I've told the police . . .'

'I know what you've told the police,' agreed Crook, his voice still soothing. 'I've access to all the statements, but that ain't what I had in mind. All you've told the police is the facts as you see them. What I want is, say, the basket of crumbs that are left over after the five thousand have fed. Tell me every single thing from the day Holles came to lunch to the time you arrived here in Cinderella's coach. And when I say everything that's just what I mean, all the remarks, the gossip, the whispers, the most casual movements or comments, any deductions you might have made for yourself—for all you know the solution lies there. Ever tried to look for a needle in a haystack?'

'I never took my sewing into a hayfield,' said Ruth composedly.

'Very short-sighted of you. You never know when that sort of experience is going to come in handy. Well, finding needles in haystacks is my hobby, just as Moss's hobby is rubbing the gilt off everybody else's gingerbread. For all I know you've already got the truth stored away in your mind, only you don't know it's the truth. Now then, shoot.'

'How long . . .?' began Ruth and he interrupted. 'I'm your life-line, sugar. The law of England may be ultra-powerful but it can't sever your life-line. We've got all the time there is. And remember, I'm one of those freaks that could win a marathon for not going to sleep if I had to. Talk all night if you've got the stuff to say, and if you're still talking by the date of the trial we'll get a postponement. Now then.'

She began, hesitatingly at first, somewhat disconcerted, as well she might be, by her legal adviser's peculiar approach. He halted her as little as he could, only sometimes, when she seemed about to dismiss an unprofitable conversation, he brought her back to some minute detail that couldn't, she was certain, have the smallest value.

'Half a minute,' he'd say, 'what happened then? No, stop and think. Who spoke next?' And so he brought her to the day of Lady Dingle's death. 'When you told them you had this migraine which caused all the trouble and said you were going to lie down, didn't anyone suggest that you mightn't be up to snuff by 3.45?'

'I don't think any of them, except Kate Waring, believed

there was such a thing as a migraine. They thought it was a whimsical phrase from a French novel. I even overheard Mrs Dingle say, "I suppose that's a fancy name for a headache." Fortunately for me, Kate knew better. Mrs Exeter sat in the sickroom at lunchtime—you know all that . . .'

'And no one offered to take over during tea? Strike you as odd? I mean, if they were preparin' to part with you, wouldn't you expect them to start gettin' into practice?'

'There was another nurse coming in on the Monday. I don't think Nurse Alexander liked it . . .'

'And when this female arrived you'd be at the end of the queue at the Labour Exchange?'

'Yes. They made a lot of that at the inquest.'

'Can't blame 'em,' said Crook. 'They're like me. They want a bit of straw to be going along with.

'Now,' he went on, 'let's come to the business of the will. Old lady didn't happen to mention it had been witnessed?'

'Not to me. I didn't even think it was strange that she should make such a point of being alone with the two old ladies. She knew I was busy, and they were obviously . . .'

'Wearin' their sitting-breeches? Quite a break for them, I shouldn't wonder, seeing no one had ever been allowed into the lioness's den before.'

'Afterwards it did seem to me a bit strange that she should have hustled them off herself. I'd have expected her to ring, but of course she didn't want them to have a chance of talking.'

'Let's get this clear. You didn't know just how much you were down for in the new will?'

'Lady Dingle didn't tell me. Frank Hardy said he overheard the family discussing it and the figure was £10,000.'

'Surprised?'

'Astounded.'

'Good. Now. You didn't know the will had been executed?'

'I didn't think about it. Lady D—'

'That's not what I asked.'

'Then—no. I didn't. At least, only by implication.'

'Meaning?'

'When Roger Dingle became so anxious to get rid of me, I smelt a rat.'

'H'm. Now, comin' to the day of Lady D.'s death. And I want the truth here and no frills. The only time you left your room between 3.30 and 4.30 was when you went to the bathroom?'

'Yes.'

'You didn't even open the old lady's door?'

'No.'

'Didn't wonder who was with her?'

'I was beyond caring.'

'Right. Now, before I go, get a load of this. Is there any single thing you've left out? Never mind which way it tells, let's have it.'

'No. There's nothing. But, Mr Crook, I've been wondering about Roger Dingle. He must have believed firstly that the will had been signed, and secondly that it was still in existence. So whoever destroyed it, if it has been destroyed, wasn't him.'

'Of course it's been destroyed, sugar,' said Crook a shade impatiently. 'What's more, I could tell you who did it. And naturally it wasn't Roger. He's a lawyer, he'd know the will could be put into effect even if it had been destroyed, but he's probably the only person in the house who did know. What I ain't so sure about,' and here his big red brow crumpled into a scowl, 'is whether the one that put the will on the fire or down the garbage chute is the same as the one that dropped the cushion on the lady's face. It don't necessarily follow. Y'see, once the will was out of the way, where was the hurry in dowsing the old lady's light? She couldn't lift a finger, couldn't speak—it's a creepy notion that she may actually have watched the destruction of the will and couldn't do a thing about it. It's a wonder she didn't die of apoplexy, if so.'

'I'm sure she didn't know,' said Ruth. 'I tried a sort of experiment . . .' She explained about the cushion. 'Dorothy Dingle came in and found me . . .'

'And couldn't keep her big mouth shut when she was in the witness box, I suppose? Still, that don't prove anything. She could have known . . . Holy smoke, I'm losing my grip. I was wondering why it should be so important to use that cushion before Holles arrived. Well, of course, the answer's as clear as the nose on my face. Now, sugar, you take that worried look off your puss and get a good night's sleep. Your Uncle Arthur's taken over. That should be a weight off your mind. No don't thank me. All part of the Arthur Crook service.'

'I dare say you've never tried sleeping on a prison bed?' suggested Ruth.

'I daresay there's worse,' replied Mr Crook, calmly. 'In 1916 I was sleeping in a kitchen with seventeen other chaps. The atmosphere got a bit thick even for me, who ain't what you might call dainty, so I found me a place under the scullery sink. You wouldn't expect there to be so much competition for that, would you. But if I'd had as many hands as a centipede has legs I swear they'd all have been trodden on by the other chaps coming up in the dark to get a cup of water.'

Snatching up his horrible brown billycock, he skipped up as gay as a mountain goat.

At the door he turned. 'One more mystery I'd like to see cleared up,' he said. 'What's Frank Hardy's stake in this?'

'He told me I'd got under his skin,' replied Ruth, indifferently.

'H'm. He told me you wouldn't look at him.'

'The point doesn't arise,' said Ruth. 'He thinks I'm responsible for my husband's death, you know?'

'I didn't. And I ain't interested in the late Appleyard. And just bear in mind that nobody else is either. We're inquirin' into the death of Lady Dingle. Any other mysterious deaths you may have been connected with don't come into this. There's times I sympathise with the ancients who sewed up their victim's mouths with needle and thread. I could do with an outsize needle myself right now.'

He had arranged to meet Frank Hardy at the King and Seven Keys in Merriton, the nearest village of any size to Dingle Halt, and when he drew up outside he found the young man waiting for him eagerly.

'How did it go?' demanded Frank.

'According to Cocker,' was Crook's slightly evasive reply. 'What's the position at the big house?'

'The Roger Dingles have gone back to London; Isobel went

immediately after the inquest. Kate's shutting up the house with the assistance of one of the old crones. I don't know what her future plans are. I suppose she'll stay within call till the trial.'

'On the premises, maybe?'

'I dare say that would be as good a plan as any, seeing she's no home. But it 'ud be lonely for her. I'd offer to stay myself, but I don't want to seem pushing . . .'

'Always wait for the lady to give the invitation. That's what my mother taught me and she was great on social behaviour. Well, it's a comfort to know she's still there. I want her to give me a hand.'

'At what?'

Crook's thick red brows shot up. He lifted the pint Frank had thoughtfully ordered. 'Just a little experiment I thought of making. Your good health—and I fancy you're going to need it.'

When he had drained the pint he strolled over to the counter and got into conversation with the landlord. As he had expected, the death of Lady Dingle and the manner of it was a plum to the neighbourhood. It was his fixed belief that you learnt more about the background of a crime from gossip at the local than from any amount of carefully-worded statements. Frank, realising he wasn't wanted for the moment, stayed where he was. Presently Crook came back, carrying a couple of pints. He summed up the situation as follows.

'Old lady a battle-axe but they don't hold it against her. Cecil a good chap, Roger a stranger. Mrs Exeter ditto. Not specially interested in Kate Waring—there's no snob like your countryman who's got independence himself, when it comes to what we ain't allowed any longer to call underlings. Young Violet—admiration flying in the face of said battle-axe and not letting herself be sliced to bits. Mrs Appleyard—the lady from London—most likely did it, a foreigner so she's no concern of theirs, but they feel grateful to her for livening things up. They don't actually want to see her swing—no malice, see?—but they won't break their hearts if she does. You know, Frank, there's no grape-vine like the one you find in villages. How come they know so much about the missing will? All that emerged in the coroner's court was that it was missing, and made ample provision for the accused. But they could pinpoint you at every turn. You haven't told them, you can bet your bottom dollar Moss hasn't, and yet I'm inclined to wonder if they don't know rather more than he does. Ah well, p'raps the Inspector married a local girl and he talks in his sleep.'

'You,' suggested Frank, politely, 'are talking through your hat.'

Crook took it off and regarded it affectionately. There wasn't another like it in the country, any more than there was another car like The Old Superb. She mightn't be everyone's cup of tea, he acknowledged cheerfully, but she was jake by him.

15

His arrival at Dingle Hall caused a minor sensation. Mrs Gusset, jamming on her felt bonnet preparatory to departure, glimpsed the bright yellow monster in the drive and marched in to Kate to say that the circus was at the door.

'The circus? What *do* you mean, Mrs Gusset?'

'That's what it looks like to me.'

'Much more likely to be the press,' said Kate, who had been pestered by reporters ever since the funeral. Even she, however, had to admit that Crook didn't look like the press. And in any case he speedily disillusioned her. But she had a fresh shock when she realised who he really was. A greater contrast to Mr Holles could scarcely be imagined.

'Nice old house,' said Crook casually, standing with his billycock in his hand. 'No central heating, though?'

Kate took the hint. 'You'd better come in, Mr . . .'

'Crook's the name. Arthur Crook. Shutting up the ancestral home?'

'None of the Dingles will want to live here,' explained Kate.

Mr Crook said heartily he didn't blame them. Not that the house was more desolate than a good many others he'd seen, just that any place that wasn't London was exile to him.

'I don't know what I can do for you,' Kate confessed. 'I've answered so many questions from the police . . .'

'I know, sugar,' said Crook soothingly. 'Only mine are going to be different.'

'Are you a friend of Mrs Appleyard's?' Kate wanted to know. 'Besides acting for her, I mean?'

'She set eyes on me for the first time this morning and she felt the same as you do. No, it was Frank Hardy pulled me into this.'

'Frank Hardy?' Her amazement slipped its leash before she could control it.

'Surprised? I don't blame you. I'd be surprised myself if I wasn't past that sort of thing. Now, that's where you may be able to help me. Just where does Master Hardy fit into the picture? He says he ain't romantically inclined, Mrs Appleyard couldn't care less about his future, or so she seems to say. So—why does he come horning in?'

'He said something the first day about having seen her before.'

'Oh so he had, but only for a few minutes nearly two years ago. He happened to be in Italy the time her husband had his accident.'

Kate's head came up with a jerk. 'And then they meet down here and Lady Dingle dies mysteriously?'

'Mr Appleyard,' said Crook firmly, 'died of a car crash when she was sittin' at home like a good wife. Lady Dingle died in her bed while Mrs A. was lyin' on hers in a state of collapse.'

'I know that's what she says . . .'

'And as her representative, naturally what she says goes for me. But you ain't answered my question about young Hardy. What I want to know is—What's in it for Walter?'

'I can't tell you much about him,' said Kate firmly.

'That seems to be the trouble. No one knows much about him. Even Mrs Dingle hadn't set eyes on him till a few weeks ago.'

'He's been a most useful guest,' Kate defended him. 'And Lady Dingle took to him from the start. She was really at her best with young people. That's one reason why she was so much attached to Ruth.'

'Happen to notice how he hit it off with Roger Dingle?'

'I don't think there was anything *to* notice. The balloon went up almost at once. He did offer to clear out . . .'

'But was persuaded to stay. I get you.'

Kate looked puzzled. 'You can't be trying to connect him with Lady Dingle's death? Why, he didn't stand to gain a thing.'

'Not directly,' acknowledged Crook. 'But where money's involved you'll generally find someone on the edge of the crowd, prepared to do a bit of pocket-pickin' when no one's lookin'.'

'Frank? But who . . . Oh no, you can't be thinking of Roger. He couldn't conceivably have any hold over him.'

'If you say so, sugar. Well, then, who?'

Kate said slowly, 'You mean, Mrs Appleyard? He knows something more than he'll admit, and he thinks if he keeps his mouth shut . . .'

'Patience can be a very payin' prospect,' said Crook. 'Mind you, I'm only feelin' in the dark the same as everyone else. But the old lady's death releases a lot of money, and it don't pay to forget that.'

'He wouldn't know anything about Roger . . . I mean there wouldn't *be* anything.'

'Maybe not, but the fact remains it was him put Mrs Appleyard wise about her share.'

'But he couldn't have known . . .'

'No?' Crook cupped a hand round a big ear and leaned forward suggestively.

'Lost his way the first night in the house, and heard quite a bit. Enough to keep him anchored here, anyway.'

'I can't believe it,' whispered Kate. 'He seems so charming . . .'

'Now come,' Crook admonished her, 'you and me weren't born yesterday. We know all is not gold that glitters and handsome is as handsome does, and it does a lot of people.'

'Are you trying to tell me that he knows more about what happened on the afternoon of Lady Dingle's death than he's told the police?'

'He knows more than he's told me,' said Crook with sudden ferocity. 'I'll never be Lord Chief Justice but I have an outside limit and, if my guess is right, he's gone right past it. I'm here to see if it is. Mind you, I don't say he knows she did it, but he knows something, and I'm goin' to get it out of him if I have to twist it out with a buttonhook. Trouble is, we've got a whale of a lot of statements that can't be supported. Mrs Appleyard says she never went near Lady D.'s room, Mrs D. says she spent the afternoon in the attics, Frank Hardy says he went right through to the billiard-room. But we can't prove any of those statements. My client could have gone into the sickroom, Hardy could have come upstairs before going along to pot the red, Mrs D. might have come downstairs a bit earlier than she let on.

'Look, let's draw up a time-table.

3.45. Nurse leaves the sickroom and goes along to the bathroom. Comin' back she hears voices—that's the Dingle brothers. All Sir Garnet. We don't have to worry about that.

3.48. (say) She hears the door of Lady Dingle's room close and assumes Mrs Appleyard's got over her migraine well enough to take over.

3.50. Mrs Exeter and Hardy come in.

4.0. (say) Nurse leaves the bathroom.

What time did she come down?'

'I do remember she was a little later than usual, say 4.10. She explained about the bath.'

'Happen to mention Mrs Appleyard?'

'I asked her who was with Lady Dingle and she said Ruth.'

'O.K. Now sometime between 4 and 4.30 Mrs Appleyard goes into the bathroom. Me, I'd say it was after Nurse came down for her tea. I don't care how ladylike you are, you can't be sick in perfect silence. How near is the bathroom to Nurse's room?'

'Next door.'

'And to reach it anyone coming from the other side of the landing would have to pass Nurse?'

'And she didn't hear or see anyone. No, I'd say Mrs Appleyard didn't go into the bathroom till, say 4.15. She didn't see anyone on the move and she didn't hear anything.'

'She wouldn't see anyone,' agreed Kate. 'Cecil had gone, Roger and Isobel were downstairs, Nurse and I were in the kitchen, Mrs Dingle was in the attics, Frank Hardy was knocking the billiard-balls about. She'd have a perfectly clear field.'

'Cuts both ways,' Crook pointed out. 'If anyone had been about they might have seen her comin' out of the bathroom. That 'ud be a help. Now, about Nurse. How much would she hear in the bathroom of movements on that floor?'

'None I should think, the way she was caterwauling,' said Kate frankly. 'It's a good thing she couldn't be heard on the floor below or Roger would have had a fit.'

'You say the floor below. That means she couldn't be heard in the billiard-room?'

'She couldn't be heard in the kitchen.'

'So it ain't likely, even if someone did open the door of the sickroom and come out and either go up the stairs or down, Nurse would hear?'

'Short of making the experiment I couldn't say,' replied Kate doubtfully, 'but I shouldn't think so.'

'Well, let's make the experiment,' said Crook. 'Nothin' against me seein' the scene of the crime, I suppose?'

'I suppose not. Though I don't see how it's going to help you.'

She led the way upstairs and opened the door of the dead woman's room. All the furniture was sheeted, the looking-glass was turned down and covered, Crook would hardly have been surprised if a skeleton had popped up from the bed.

'Now,' he suggested, 'show me the bathroom. Ah! Quite a way.'

'Lady Dingle didn't like the sound of running water, she said it disturbed her. That's why she'd never have a basin in her room.'

'Well, sugar, you go along and sing nice and hearty and presently tell me how much you've heard of what I was doing.'

He heard the bathroom door close and then a voice began to chant:

'If I were the only girl in the world and you were the only boy . . .'

It stopped and he shouted, 'Keep it up, sugar.'

'I don't know the rest of the words. I'll sing something else.' She began Jingle-bells. Crook walked around humming, 'Nothing else would matter in the world today, We could go on loving in the same old way, A garden of Eden, just made for two, With nothing to mar our joy.'

Still singing, he crossed the landing, ran buoyantly down

the back stairs, poked his nose into the kitchen, discovered the billiard-room, came back to the staircase foot, hesitated there an instant and then came bounding up the stairs again and went into the sickroom and came out again, closing the door.

'O.K.' he called.

Kate opened the bathroom door and came out.

'Let's have it,' said Crook. 'What did you hear?'

Kate looked doubtful. 'Nothing special.'

'And I wasn't bein' noticeably quiet. Fact is, sugar, anyone could have gone walking around. Nurse wouldn't have heard. You didn't stop singin', did you?'

'No.' Kate looked startled.

'I didn't think you had.'

'What does that prove?'

'What I've been thinkin' for some time. That young Hardy didn't go to the billiard-room right away like he said.'

'You mean, he came upstairs first? How can you be sure?'

'That's the worst of amateurs. They always give themselves away. Which staircase did he generally use?'

'Oh, the back one, always. It was much nearer his room. Actually, I don't think anyone but Roger and his wife and occasionally Isobel used the front stairs.'

'So he could easy come up without being seen? It 'ud be natural enough for him to want to freshen up after a walk, and Roger was in the downstairs cloakroom. So he runs up the back stairs and—maybe he sees someone going into Lady's D.'s room.'

'But then he'd know it wasn't Ruth . . .'

'I said someone,' Crook pointed out, dryly.

There was a long pause. 'Yes, I see,' agreed Kate. 'And that's when he offered to try and bring you in. Mr Crook, have you any proof of any of this?'

'Not a sausage,' agreed Crook, cheerfully. 'Only—I know he was up on this floor, and if he ain't got something to hide, why ain't he come out with the fact? Could be he knows it *wasn't* Ruth Appleyard, and he don't want her to hang for something she didn't do.'

'Then it must have been—but, Mr Crook, she was up in the attics. Or don't you believe that, either?'

'I'm darn sure she was in the attics. She had to be somewhere, hadn't she? And she wasn't with her husband, she
wasn't with you, she wasn't in the bathroom because Nurse was
in there singing fit to bust the band by all accounts . . .'

'Flat,' agreed Kate, succinctly.

'And if she'd been in her own room how come she never
heard anything? No, she was in the attics all right. Only—how
long was she there? And where did she go when she came
down?'

'She noticed there wasn't a light under the sickroom door,'
Kate reminded him.

'Landing light was off, too, I understand?'

'Yes. I hadn't had time to replace the bulb.'

'Well, that's her story. She's got no more proof it's true than
—anyone else.'

'If the light was off in the sickroom, Lady Dingle must have
been dead when Dorothy opened the door.'

'If,' repeated Crook. 'I told you—there's no proof.'

'About the light?' Kate looked puzzled.

'I mean, there's no proof the old lady had passed in her
checks *before* Mrs Dingle entered the room.'

Crook had arranged to meet Frank at another inn, called
The Sportsman and His Dog on the further side of Dingle
Halt, and once again Frank was waiting for him.

'Well?' he enquired eagerly. 'Have you learnt anything?'

'You've got a nerve,' said Crook. 'And you can lay off the
innocent stunt. You've told enough lies to get yourself the
wrong side of Newgate Gaol. When I undertake a case I don't
expect to be double-crossed by my own side. Now let's have a
bit of truth for a change. First of all, *whose side are you on*?'

'Ruth's, of course,' Frank sounded indignant.

'I wonder why? Because, whatever the facts are about Lady
D.'s death, she'll be nicely padded when all this is over, and
I've got her off the rope? Pipe down. Seeing truth ain't your
strong suit, I'll do the talking for a bit. And I'll tell *you* what
happened. And it's no sense you trying to make out it ain't so,
because I've been down to the house myself, and smelt out the
lie of the land.'

Crook, angry, could be as formidable as a dive-bomber, as

141

Frank now had the opportunity to appreciate. Nevertheless he strove to temporise.

'If you've been listening to Kate . . .' he began.

'Why,' burst forth Crook, 'what does Kate know?'

'So far as I'm concerned, nothing. Only you were so thundering anxious to meet her . . .'

'I'm thundering anxious to get my client acquitted. That's what I'm here for. The rest of you can swing from lamp-posts till the flesh falls off your bones, for all I care. First, you made the sort of mistake tiros always do. You didn't actually tell a black lie, you refrained from telling the truth.'

'About?' Frank hung on to his temper, realising that he was no match for Crook in this (or probably any) mood.

'Your movements after you came in. Oh, I don't say you didn't go along to the billiard-room like you said, only you didn't go there right away.'

'No?'

'No. You came up the back stairs. Though how there were so many of you beetling around and none of you managed to meet beats me.'

'Who says I did anything of the kind?'

'I do. Come to that, you told me yourself. Because, y'see, you heard Nursie bawlin' in her bath, *and you can't hear that in the billiard-room*. Hell, you can't hear it on that lower floor at all. Now let's talk a bit of sense. It'll make a nice change. What were you doin' on that staircase?'

'I always used that staircase,' retorted Frank, defensively.

'And you saw X. go into Lady D.'s room? Or had she finished the job?'

'I saw someone go into the sickroom,' Frank sounded desperate.

'Happen to notice where she came from?'

'I . . .?'

'All right, all right, let me say it for you. She came down the attic stairs, didn't she?'

'Of course not.' Frank was caught off guard. 'Why on earth should she be up there?'

'I see,' said Crook. 'So it was Mrs Appleyard?'

'Yes. But, Crook, I only saw her go in. I didn't stop. She

may have come out again the next minute. She was at the end of her tether. How could I tell the police the facts? They wouldn't have given her the benefit of the doubt for five minutes. And someone else may have gone along later, you know that's true . . .'

'I'm like the White Queen,' said Crook, 'I can believe six impossible things before breakfast, but even I have my limits. So she went in and nothing happened and she strayed out again and then someone else went in, noticing the light was out— come on, let's have it. What was your arrangement with her? Fifty-fifty of anything she got under the old lady's will?'

Frank sprang to his feet, but Crook pulled him roughly down again.

'We ain't playin' this at the Lyceum,' he pointed out. 'All I'm askin' is—what's your motive? You're not in love with her, you told me so yourself. You're risking perjury, because you'll be asked to repeat your statement at the trial, tellin' the truth, the whole truth, which you certainly haven't done to date . . .'

'You're overlooking one thing,' said Frank, who had turned very pale. 'It's my word against hers. I can't prove a thing.'

'And you were darned anxious the police shouldn't know you'd been upstairs that afternoon. I wonder why that was. You didn't have to tell them you'd seen anyone go into the death-chamber. But no, you played it the hard way. You stuck to it that you hadn't been up the stairs. Maybe you had a reason for that you've forgotten to mention?'

'It must be perfectly obvious I didn't stand to gain a thing from Lady Dingle's death . . .'

And Crook said again, as he'd said before, 'Well, not directly. But silence can be a very expensive commodity. Which of them has discovered that, Frank Hardy? Ruth Appleyard? **Or Dorothy Dingle?** Come on—let's have it. I'm waiting.'

16

It had been said of Crook that he couldn't like grass much, since he never let it grow under his feet . . . After leaving the discomfited Frank Hardy he put on his thinking-cap—he stuck to the old-fashioned phrases of his youth—and pretty soon he had been in touch with both the Dingle brothers with a suggestion that met with acquiescence from one and scarcely veiled antagonism from the other. When, however, he had got his own way, as he had intended all along the line, he paid Ruth another flying visit.

'Just a check-up,' he said, putting one or two fresh points that had occurred to him. 'Incidentally, you ought to take up one of these memory courses when you've got a little time on your hands. How come you forgot Hardy had seen you goin' into the old lady's room?'

'He didn't,' declared Ruth, steadfastly. 'I never left my room that afternoon except to go to the bathroom. If he did see anyone going in, it wasn't me.'

'H'm. I'd be happier about this case if I didn't feel I was bein' double-crossed left, right and centre. You stick to that?'

'Yes.'

'You could,' said Crook, carefully, 'have mentioned it before.'

'Frank said he wasn't going to tell anyone. He got you because he believes in his heart I did it.'

'There's one more question,' said Crook, 'and let's have a direct answer this time. Has he made any proposals to you —and I don't mean matrimonial? If things turn out the way my cases mostly do you're going to have quite a nice little nest-egg. Any suggestion from Frank Hardy that he might help to hatch it?'

Ruth looked furious. 'Of course not.'

'No of course about it. Between you, you've suppressed enough evidence to earn a five year sentence apiece, and on my soul,' exploded Crook, 'I don't know why I don't leave you to get it, except that as a ratepayer I don't see why I should have to support the pair of you in five years' unproductive idleness.'

He blew out again like a storm-wind and prepared himself for the final act.

In London Roger took up the telephone and called his brother.

'I take it you've heard from this maniac who's acting for Mrs Appleyard?' he began. 'What do you make of the fellow?'

'A thruster,' said Cecil. 'A last-ditcher man. Probably the best chap Mrs Appleyard could have found. He came over to see us when he was down here. Vi said later that, if ever she was arrested for murder, she hoped I'd remember his name.'

'He spoke to me of fresh evidence not yet available to the police,' continued Roger. 'It all sounds exceedingly irregular to me. Did he drop any hint . . .?'

'I certainly got the impression he was keeping an ace up his sleeve,' acknowledged Cecil.

'A fellow like that wouldn't recognise a pack of cards with fewer than five aces,' was Roger's disdainful retort. 'He's invited me and Dorothy down to Dingle Hall for what he calls a reconstruction of the crime. There's no doubt about it, he's an exhibitionist to the heels of his abominable yellow shoes.'

'Good luck to him, if Mrs Appleyard is innocent, as Vi is convinced she is.'

'Violet! What's that called? Feminine intuition?'

'She swears Ruth was really fond of Mamma, apart from expectations.'

'No doubt she'll tell you she was fond of her father and husband and look what happened to them. Very well then, we shall meet tomorrow afternoon. I'm bringing Holles with me; a chap like Crook could pick your pockets while he was shaking hands.'

'What's cooking?' asked Nurse Alexander, when Crook rang her up. 'Are you going to uncover the villain? Yes, of course I'll come. Mind you, I have my own ideas, but I dare say yours are better.'

'Well,' murmured Crook, kindly, 'it's my job,' and rang off, having arranged to pick her up in the Superb on his way to Dingle Hall.

Frank Hardy was given no choice. 'Curtain rises on the last act Tuesday four o'clock,' he was told succinctly. 'If you're afraid of missing your train, you can come along with me and Nursie.'

'It sounds a rum sort of tea-party,' was Violet's comment. 'Or is Mr Crook going to drop something in the evil-doer's cup? If you take my advice, darling, you'll take a gun along. I don't trust any of that crowd as far as I could kick them, and in my present state that wouldn't be far.'

When they arrived Kate had got a handsome fire burning in the library where, as if by tacit consent, Roger and his family, with Kate and Mr Holles, seated themselves in a stubborn clump, leaving Crook with Nurse Alexander and Frank to take three chairs on the rim of the assembly.

'Caste distinctions,' reflected Crook, thinking that they looked defiant rather than aloof.

'I wish to put it on record,' said Mr Holles at once, 'that I am here under protest. This meeting is most irregular. If you have any fresh information you should give it to the authorities.'

Replied Crook amiably, 'In about five minutes—or possibly ten, depends on how fast we get on—you'll have a chance of doing my job for me. I see there's a telephone nice and handy.' He nodded towards the instrument that stood on a bracket near the door. 'Now, hold your breath everyone, because this is going to give you a shock. Hardy here has been concealing a vital clue, under the amateur's impression that you can use your own judgment when you're dealin' with the police. Now then, Frank, let's have it.'

Frank Hardy, looking like a man expecting to be shot at dawn, said miserably, 'Mr Crook thinks I should let you all know that I didn't go straight to the billiard-room when I came back that afternoon. I went upstairs . . .'

'Then why not say so?' snapped Roger.

But Holles, quicker on the draw, said at once, 'And by so doing you obtained a piece of evidence that you have seen fit to conceal? I take it it concerns Mrs Appleyard.'

'Everything we're sayin' this afternoon concerns Mrs Appleyard,' agreed Crook, a little impatiently. 'Come on Frank, we haven't all day.'

'I suppose,' continued Frank desperately, 'he has his own reasons for wanting everyone to know that—in fact—I saw Mrs Appleyard leave her room and go into Lady Dingle's.'

The effect of this statement was as impressive as a rocket suddenly exploding in their midst.

Mr Holles leaned forward. 'You mean to say, you have been deliberately suppressing the fact?'

'Well, of course that's what he means,' said Crook easily. 'To hear you, anyone 'ud think you'd never run up against this kind of thing before. But I know better. Great snakes, man, you've been in the legal racket for forty years.'

Holles, disregarding this, continued, 'And, knowing that Mrs Appleyard was making a false statement, you held your tongue, thereby becoming an accessory to the crime?'

'You're riding in front of the hounds,' Crook warned him. 'Mrs Appleyard ain't been convicted of any crime to date.'

'If Mr Hardy did, in fact, see Mrs Appleyard enter Lady Dingle's room, I can see no point in this meeting. I take it he is prepared to repeat the statement in the witness-box?'

'The Defence 'ull make mincemeat of him if he does,' retorted Crook, unexpectedly. 'Y'see, I don't accept Hardy's statement. No, Frank, I'm not calling you a liar, only, since you got a bit muddled the first time you told your story, it could be you're still a mite confused. Now, think. When you saw this apparition, did you call out or anything?'

'No. Anyway, there was no time. I only saw her for a split second.'

'And the lady didn't hail you?'

'I doubt if she could have seen me where I was standing. I was looking across obliquely from the passage. You wouldn't see anyone there, unless you came halfway across the landing.'

'And even then, with the light off—it was off, wasn't it?'

'Yes.'

'Even then you might not see anyone, or, even if you could, you mightn't be sure who it was?'

'No. Except that I don't think any of the other men in the house ever used the back stairs.'

'Still, there was nothing to prevent them, and if you said you hadn't been there it 'ud be possible for it to have been someone else?'

Mr Holles made an impatient movement. 'Really, Mr Crook, no one is challenging Mr Hardy's presence at the head of the back staircase.'

'Quite,' agreed Crook. 'The point I'm tryin' to establish is that with the landin' light off you couldn't swear to his identity. And so I'm asking him how *he* could swear to the identity of the woman he saw leaving Mrs Appleyard's room. Well, Frank, any answer to that?'

There was a quick gasp from the assembly. Then Frank said, 'But—but—she came out of Mrs Appleyard's room . . . so naturally I took it for granted.'

'Exactly. You took it for granted. And if you'd seen me come out of her room would you have taken for granted— never mind, you needn't answer that one.'

Mr Holles, leaning back in his chair, inquired, 'Is this the case the defence proposes to take into court, Crook? With no more proof?'

'A hell of a lot more proof,' said Crook vigorously. 'That's why we're all here today at approximately the time it all happened. I'm goin' to suggest a little experiment, and if anyone refuses to play ball you can't blame me if I draw the obvious conclusions. Now I want all you gents to stop here till I give the word, the ladies to come upstairs with me.'

'This is exceedingly irregular,' protested Mr Holles for the second time, but Cecil chimed in, 'I imagine we're all prepared to give Mr Crook such assistance as we can. It would be a shocking thing if Mrs Appleyard were to be convicted of a crime of which she is not, in fact, guilty.'

'Someone is guilty,' said Roger, in wooden tones.

'I get you,' observed Crook. 'Naturally you'd like to think it was the cuckoo in the nest. But even cuckoos have a right to a square deal.'

Roger glanced at Holles, who said, 'If you are prepared to assist Mr Crook, I shall raise no objection. But it all seems to me unnecessarily—melodramatic.'

'That's the way with murder,' said Crook. 'Now then, if the ladies 'ull come with me. Keep the door shut till I give the word, Frank, and then come up the stairs the way you did that afternoon.'

'What is all this about?' exclaimed Dorothy, uneasily, as they mounted the main staircase.

'I'm trying to save a girl's life,' Crook reminded her. 'Now, Nurse, do you mind setting the scene? Run the water, switch on the light in the room that was yours—that's Mrs Appleyard's, isn't it—Lady Dingle's door was ajar—' He moved about as cool as a cucumber, as if he hadn't a care in the world and the whole of eternity at his disposal. When everything was in order he shouted, 'Right, Frank,' and heard the library door open. Feet came up the back staircase. Frank came first, with Cecil right at his heels. Mr Holles, still protesting, followed with Roger.

'Stop just about where you did that night, Frank,' Crook ordered him. 'Now, is that the only light that was on?'

'Yes. I hadn't turned on the passage light. The switch is a couple of paces to the left.'

'Good. Now take a look round and make sure the scene's set right. Bathroom door open a crack and light showing, water running, Nurse's door ditto. Mrs A.'s door standing ajar, but no light, Lady Dingle's door drawn to, but a light showing beneath it. O.K.?'

'Yes,' said Frank.

'Right. Come on out, lady. We're all set.' Turning to the group beside him he added, 'Keep your eyes peeled and be ready to tell me afterwards everything you see.'

Someone appeared at the door of Ruth Appleyard's room,

came out, closed the door softly, took a few paces to Lady Dingle's room, pushed that door wide and entered. The door then closed with its characteristic sound. Frank turned along the passage, switching on the light as he did so, and disappeared into his own room, Nurse left her room, like an actress awaiting her cue, walked into the bathroom, closed and bolted the door, turned off the water. A minute later they heard a splashing sound and then her voice uplifted.

'If I were the only girl in the world and you were the only boy . . .'

'It's quite true,' murmured Crook, 'she does sing flat. Go on, Frank,' he added, 'do your stuff.'

Frank came marching back and ran down the stairs. 'Tell us when you can't hear the orchestra,' called Crook. Frank went along the passage, hesitated, listened, and said, 'I'm out of earshot now.'

'So you see,' observed Crook to his audience, 'he couldn't possibly have heard her if he'd been in the billiard-room. All right, Nurse,' he shouted. 'We'll be getting back to a fire. Collect the ladies and bring 'em down the front stairs. I don't want anyone to die of pneumonia on my account.'

'Well,' he enquired as they reached the floor below, 'what did you see? Mr Dingle?'

'I saw nothing out of the way,' snapped Roger, 'simply Mrs Appleyard's stand-in leaving her room and entering my mother's.'

'I should have put it another way,' apologised Crook. 'What I meant is—who did you see?'

'I told you—Mrs Appleyard's understudy, if you prefer the word.'

'I'm looking for a name,' explained Crook, patiently. 'There were four ladies—well, three, since Nurse was in the bathroom —your wife, your sister and Miss Waring. Which of the three did you see go out of one room and enter the other?'

'I couldn't possibly tell in that light—' he stopped. 'I understand now what you were getting at. You certainly have your wits about you,' he added grudgingly.

'I thought you'd get there sooner or later,' Crook congratulated him. 'Any views?' He turned to Cecil.

'No,' said Cecil. 'They'd all look pretty much alike in the same sort of clothes with so little illumination. You've made your point, Crook, there's not a doubt about that. The utmost Hardy can say is that he saw a woman whom he took to be Mrs Appleyard go into my mother's room.'

17

They reached the door of the library and went gratefully in towards the fire. The four women were already seated.

'It was Isobel,' said Dorothy. 'Did you recognise her?'

'All this kind of thing gets us very little further,' said Mr Holles. 'You have not yet provided an iota of proof, Crook, that the figure Mr Hardy saw was *not* Mrs Appleyard. I feel certain the jury will want to know why anyone else should have been in her room at that hour.'

'I thought we might take the examination a little further and see if we could find out,' agreed Crook, pleasantly. 'We know who it couldn't have been. It couldn't have been Mrs Exeter, because she's got an alibi. She was with her brother.'

'And I was in the attics,' said Dorothy, sharply, 'and Kate was in the kitchen.'

'And Nurse was in the bath. Well, it so happens she's the only person who can prove her whereabouts. Nobody saw you go up to the attics, Mrs Dingle, you didn't mention to anyone you were going there, you didn't find the thing you say you were looking for.'

'And I suppose Kate can't *prove* she was in the kitchen since there was no one else there,' began Dorothy, but once again Holles threw himself into the breach.

'It would be more to the point if Mr Crook could adduce some acceptable reason why either of you ladies should have been in Mrs Appleyard's room. Well, Crook?'

'It's perfectly simple,' said Crook. 'They both knew Mrs A. had collapsed at lunch-time. It might have occurred to either of them that she mightn't be fit for duty by four o'clock. Either of them might have peeped in to make sure . . .'

'It would never have occurred to me,' said Dorothy, frankly. 'I regarded it as an ordinary headache from which I should expect Mrs Appleyard to recover in a couple of hours.'

'But, you see, you can't prove that,' Crook insisted. 'It would have been possible for X.—let's say X.—to take a look-see, find Mrs Appleyard still *hors de combat* and, with the best will in the world, decide to relieve her of her watch. At that stage I'm quite prepared to believe X. had no ill intentions towards Lady Dingle at all. This crime hasn't any of the hall-marks of premeditation. It was committed on the spur of the moment, I'm pretty sure of that, under some tremendous impulse. You see, the way I read it is that, after X. got inside that room, she realised something or discovered something or something happened that made Lady Dingle a danger to her. Once we know what that something is we're more than halfway home.'

'This is the merest guesswork,' protested Holles.

'Detection's largely guesswork. Remember Artemus Ward? Get the evidence and then arrange it the way you like. It's mainly guesswork that Mrs Appleyard dumped the cushion on the old lady's face.'

'And are we, then, to assume that this helpless, insensible old lady did something to fill her companion with such fear or hatred that she could see no way out of her dilemma short of murder? Really, Crook, is that what you are asking us to believe?'

'Something uncommonly like it,' Crook agreed. 'You see, there's one thing you've overlooked. You don't positively know that on that particular afternoon at that particular time the old lady was insensible, and if, in point of fact, she was not . . .'

A clamour arose all about him. He caught the words 'preposterous,' 'fantastic' and once again 'melodramatic'. He waited till some of the dust had settled, then said coolly, 'I don't speak without the book. I've been talking to Freeman and also to a buddy of mine from Undertakers Alley—Harley Street to you—and they all say you can't dogmatise in cases like this. Freeman had warned you from the start that Lady Dingle might come round at any time, for a minute, for an hour, for an indefinite period. There need be no warning, no special symptoms. It 'ud be like someone making a comeback after any serious illness involvin' a similar state. Say, for the sake of argument, that on this particular afternoon some development took place to make X. realise that Lady D. was, so to speak, once more "in residence" . . .'

'All this is sheer supposition,' protested Roger.

'I know.' Crook sounded deceptively mild. 'But we have to find some reason for this attack. People don't pick up cushions and smother old women for the fun of the thing or as a scientific experiment. X. had some good reason for wanting to stop the old lady's mouth. And I can only think of one reason, which was that she'd suddenly returned to the world and returned with a knowledge X. couldn't afford to let other people know.'

He sat back, his big brown eyes passing anxiously from face to face.

'And what,' enquired Mr Holles at last, 'do you suggest this mysterious knowledge was?'

'Since you ask me, I'd say it had to do with the missing will. Y'see, even if in law it ain't been established that it was destroyed, all present, being sensible chaps, know it couldn't have taken wings and flown over the houses. And it ain't on the premises and no one posted it, and it wasn't entrusted to anyone because, like Mrs 'Arris, there ain't no sich person. No, it was destroyed and my bet 'ud be it was burned under the old lady's eyes, by someone who didn't think there was a witness.'

He'd got everyone's attention now. They were like puppets on a string.

'In a moment,' said Roger slowly, 'you're going to tell us who that person was. Let me remind you, even if we admit the probability that the will has been destroyed, criminally destroyed,' he added in more powerful tones, 'we are in no position to say who was responsible. No one knows that.'

'On the contrary,' said Crook, 'two people know for certain and I should say there were three. The person who did the job, me and A. N. Other.'

'A. N. Other being . . .'

'I should have thought that stuck out a mile,' said Crook bluntly. 'The late Lady Dingle, of course. Otherwise, why was she smothered that afternoon? To shut her mouth . . .'

'You're assuming she knew—you haven't the ghost of a right to assume anything of the kind.'

'You're assuming she couldn't know, but equally you've no grounds for that. Remember the horror story of the man in a catalepsy watching his family prepare for the funeral, seeing, hearing and not able to make a sign to prove he was alive? That must have given more people nightmares than Dracula. So far as I remember they got him right inside the coffin . . . Because Lady D. couldn't make any sign it don't prove she didn't know, and if she hadn't known something and made that obvious to X., she might be lyin' upstairs in that sheeted bogy-hole this very minute.'

'Very ingenious,' said Roger in a tone of icy composure. 'Now perhaps you will tell us who destroyed the will.'

'There can't be any two opinions about that,' said Crook. There's only one person it could have been. There's only one person who knew the names—or at all events, one name of the witnesses. Now, Miss Waring, let's hear you explain to the meeting how you knew Mrs Archer was one of the signatories, unless you'd seen the completed will.'

If a wave of icy water had broken over the assembly they could not have registered shock more emphatically. Kate cried out, Dorothy caught her hand. Holles leaned forward to say imperatively, 'Miss Waring, be advised by me and don't allow yourself to become involved in an argument. This man is not the police—'

'We can have them in, if you like,' offered Crook obligingly. 'I'm quite agreeable.'

Roger said, 'I agree with Mr Holles. This charge is fantastic.' But there was apprehension below the quiet voice.

'In my opinion,' said Cecil, 'Miss Waring should be given an opportunity of refuting it, for Mrs Appleyard's sake as well as her own. Yes, Roger—' as his brother opened his lips to protest. 'I hardly think Mr Crook would make this statement unless he is prepared to implement it in court, so if it could be cleared up now it would be to the advantage of us all. Perhaps, Mr Crook, you will explain what reasons you have for the accusation you've just made.'

They sat in a row all staring him out of countenance. But Crook was not in the least discomposed.

'Miss Waring told the police that the name of one of the

ladies who called and who, we now know, witnessed the will was Archer. She said she heard her friend call her that. But the friend happened to be her sister and you don't generally call your sister by her married name. You say Susan or Jemima or—Kate. And she couldn't have heard that anyway *because she never met either of them*. Mrs Appleyard let them in and nobody saw them out.'

'Then I suppose I made a mistake and Lady Dingle mentioned the name to me,' said Kate, with a little breathless laugh for her own forgetfulness.

'But she didn't call them anything but Dilly and Dally,' Crook reminded her. 'Why, she said it wouldn't surprise her to know those were their real names. Had you forgotten? And it was a cash transaction, so you couldn't have seen the name on a counterfoil. No, Miss Waring, if you can show I'm barking up the wrong tree you ought to join the Magicians' Guild.' His pitiless brown eyes raked the speechless assembly. 'Which of you went running with your tongue out to tell her her legacy had been cut from £3,000 to £500?'

'I didn't tell her anything of the kind,' protested Dorothy. 'I simply warned her that Mrs Appleyard had stolen a march on us all. I thought she had a right to know. Did you really burn it, Kate?' she added in tones of awed admiration. 'Not that I blame you. It's what I meant to do myself if I could have found it.'

'Nonsense,' exclaimed Roger loudly. 'You don't know what you're saying, Dorothy.'

'Women aren't like us,' put in Crook with unexpected mildness. 'They don't have our natural respect for the law. To them it's all a lot of ballyhoo. Yes, I believe she would.'

'Nonsense,' said Roger again. 'She would have done nothing of the kind. As a barrister's wife . . .'

Dorothy laughed. It was a shocking sound. 'Do you suppose that's given me any respect for the law? In a way, Roger, I hope she did know.'

The situation was getting rapidly out of hand.

'The fact remains,' said Roger, looking very white, 'you did not destroy the document. Mr Crook has accused Kate of doing so. I hope, Kate, you'll have the sense to say nothing further.

For one thing, you can't really believe such an act would achieve anything. The will had been drawn up by Mr Holles, we know it had been duly executed, we can get affidavits from the two ladies, Mrs Archer and her sister, I've spoken to Dr Freeman and there is no question of my mother being *non compos mentis* . . .'

He got no further. Kate burst in like a whirlwind. 'You mean, it's all been for nothing, everything I've done? That Cecil's life can still be ruined by this infamous will? A thousand pounds, indeed! It's no better than robbery.'

'Ruined?' exclaimed Cecil as amazed as she. 'How can it be? I've got Violet and presently I shall have our child. They are my life now.'

'But you'll lose the estate,' clamoured Kate. 'Do you think I haven't always realised that that's the first thing in your life? I knew it more than twenty years ago when I refused to come away with you and risk your being disinherited. Risk? It was an absolute certainty. Your mother would never have forgiven you for marrying your sister's governess.'

'I think she would,' said Cecil, white as a sheet at the recollection of that ancient pain. 'But, if she hadn't, I could have got something else.'

'Perhaps,' agreed Kate, 'but you would never have forgiven me for costing you so dear.'

'Things you get cheap are seldom worth having,' insisted Cecil. 'Violet was faced by the same considerations but she didn't hesitate.'

'And,' said Kate, trembling, 'if Roger's right it's no good, because you've lost the estate. You won't be able to keep it up, not if this last will holds.'

'Don't you see, Kate, that doesn't matter any more. The estate was only of paramount importance when I had nothing else. What I've got now is worth a hundred properties. Violet—'

'Violet! Violet! Is that all you think of?' cried Kate in a fiercely despairing tone. 'Oh Cecil, how you've changed. Twenty years ago . . .'

'Have you ever wondered what the intervening twenty years did to me, after I'd realised you didn't believe in me enough to chance your future as my wife?' Cecil demanded. Both seemed to have forgotten their audience.

'Not believe in you? I, who've never had a thought apart from you for a quarter of a century? I, who was prepared to face imprisonment to get you your just share of the property? I . . .? But if, after everything, that last will stands . . .'

'Mr Crook—' Roger was on his feet— 'I can't pretend to be anything but horrified by the way you've misused your professional status. You have deliberately tried to trick Miss Waring into an admission of guilt—you must realise that you have nothing but your own hypothesis to put before the authorities, and in any case we are discussing my mother's death, not the destruction of the will, of which even now we have no definite proof . . .'

'Don't try and play the bogy man with me,' said Crook, contemptuously. 'If you're suggesting I've behaved as no gentleman should, I've never pretended to be a gent. I should have expected you to see that for yourself. And try and get this into your head. I'm not concerned with anyone in this case except my client. I don't deal in human beings. If you have your way, this girl's going to hang, no doubt about that.'

'And if you have your way someone else will.'

'If you're trying to suggest *I* was in Lady Dingle's room,' said Kate, recovering herself, 'you're wasting your time. Oh, it's a fine show you've put up, Mr Crook, but—*I was in the kitchen*.'

'Ah, but when? That's the point. At 3.30, you told the police, and maybe that's the truth. But—not at 3.50 or you wouldn't have known about the busted bulb. That didn't conk out till 3.45.' He looked across to Nurse Alexander.

'That's right,' said Nurse, hard as a concrete wall.

'And not at 3.55 or you wouldn't have heard Nurse singing—flat. You remember. O.K., Nurse. She was right, you know. You couldn't hear in the kitchen—we proved that when I came over and we made our experiment—and Frank here proved it again five minutes ago. And not at four o'clock, for Frank says there was no one stirring when he came down, which is why he went along to knock the balls about. Right, Frank?'

'Right,' agreed Frank, in a voice that matched Nurse Alexander's. 'There wasn't a soul to be seen anywhere.'

Nurse Alexander startled them all by saying suddenly, 'No scones.'

Crook turned. 'Come again, sugar.'

'We always had scones for tea, every day that I was in the house except *that* afternoon. Miss Waring used to toss them up and serve them hot. But that day it was only currant bread.'

'The best housekeeper on earth can't be in two places at once,' Crook pointed out. 'Well, Miss Waring, let's have it. If you weren't in the kitchen and you weren't in Lady Dingle's room—and you can't have been in your own room or you'd have heard something of what was going on—*where were you?*'

Roger pushed back his chair with a harsh sound. 'Don't answer any questions, Kate,' he commanded. 'We've had enough of this—farce.' He turned to Crook, his face dark with anger.

'You're not going to persuade any jury that after thirty years of devoted service, Miss Waring was going to turn on a helpless old woman,' he assured him.

'Devoted service?' repeated Crook, derisively. 'Odd devotion to cheat an old woman who was in her power by destroying the will when she couldn't prevent it. And you call that farce? Are you aware there's a woman's life at stake?' His anger rolled over them like a sudden burst of thunder.

His rage seemed contagious. Now Kate, thrusting aside Roger's detaining hand, said, '*I* cheated her? And what did she do to me? First, she wrecked my happiness, and for the next twenty years I was her bond-woman, her slave—yes, Roger, her slave—and then along comes Ruth Appleyard, who's had the sort of life I can't even imagine, and overnight she's the pet, the favourite, she has the best room, the most attention. Of course, I hated her. I hated them both.'

'That's the truth, anyway,' confirmed Nurse, stolidly. 'I always knew it. I saw you watching her when you didn't realise anyone was noticing. I was glad it was Ruth Appleyard and not you that shared the job with me. She was different. When Mr Dingle told her she wouldn't be wanted any more, it wasn't just the money she thought of, but the old lady coming round and asking for her and hearing she'd lit out when things got difficult. She'd never have done such a thing, you take my word.'

'Unfortunately for Mrs Appleyard,' observed Roger 'that is what a court of law won't do.'

'Don't say another word, Kate,' exclaimed Isobel, speaking for the first time. 'You've said too much as it is.'

'I haven't said anything that isn't true,' flared Kate. 'Of course I detested her. I'm human, aren't I? But at least you can believe this. I didn't burn the will because she'd cheated me—I was used to that—but she meant to cheat Cecil, too, after stealing his life for so long. After twenty years she was going to cheat him of the estate: did you think I'd sit by and see that happen, after what I'd paid all that time? Of course not. And Ruth was to profit at your expense, that seemed to make it worse. But at least I could prevent that, or so I thought. Oh well!' She dropped back in her chair; the fire that informed her seemed to die down like a guttering candle. 'It seems I've wasted my efforts.'

'Not quite,' said Crook, dryly.

'You mean, Ruth won't hang? That's all you care about, isn't it?'

'It's all I'm here for,' said Crook.

'Mind you, I don't admit anything, and there's nothing you can prove.'

'I ain't the police. You were reminded of that just now. I don't have to prove anything. It's for the prosecution to prove beyond all reasonable doubt that Ruth Appleyard murdered Lady Dingle. Well, no jury's going to dare bring in a verdict of guilty in the light of the story I'm going to tell. Tell me, Miss Waring, what did the old lady really say that afternoon?'

'She didn't say anything,' cried Kate. 'She was unconscious.'

'How come you're so sure if you weren't there?'

'She never recovered consciousness,' repeated Kate, steadily. 'Ask Nurse.'

Nurse Alexander sat up abruptly. 'But she did,' she whispered. 'At least . . .'

'Give, sugar,' pleaded Crook. 'I didn't think you'd hold out on me.'

'I've only just thought. When I came upstairs, after Mrs Dingle called me, the old lady had a fold of the counterpane between her fingers. Don't you see what that means? She must have recovered to some extent—it doesn't prove she was conscious, of course, but—she could have been. She'd moved her hand—it was lying like something made of wax when I left her. Don't you see what that means? She'd moved . . .'

'It's funny you didn't mention it to the police,' flared Kate. 'Who saw it, besides you?' She looked defiantly round the circle. 'Don't you see, she's in league with them? She doesn't mind what she says to bolster up his case.'

'I haven't got a case,' repeated Crook patiently. 'All I have to do is show it could have been someone else. Y'know, it's what I've always said. Murder's an amateur's crime. They all make one mistake. This time it was turning out the light. It's not natural to leave a sick woman in the dark. But, of course, if you've just committed a murder you could have your reasons . . .'

Holles pushed back his chair with a violent, grating sound.

'You wouldn't listen to me,' he said in harsh tones to Roger, 'when I warned you to have nothing to do with this— charade. I hope you're satisfied with the result. As for you, Miss Waring, you would be well advised to answer no question from the authorities without a solicitor in attendance.'

Kate was also on her feet. 'If Mr Crook imagines he's built up a case against me I can assure you all he's mistaken. What can he prove? Nothing. He says I wasn't in the kitchen, therefore I must have been in Lady Dingle's room. I say I was never there that afternoon, and I defy him to provide any proof. No one here will believe his ridiculous accusations.' She turned to them scornfully—Roger, Cecil, Isobel. 'None of you will support him, I know.'

But the eyes that met hers for an instant and then turned away brought her no reassurance. She caught her breath.

'Has he bewitched you all? By a trick? Don't you see, he doesn't care who hangs so long as his client goes free.'

No one moved, no one spoke, and she remembered a dreadful story she had once read of a man, imprisoned in an icy dungeon, who became suddenly aware that the darkness was pierced with innumerable points of light as the rats came stealing from their hiding-places to surround their prey.

'Don't stare at me like that,' she said, unsteadily. 'I tell you, I didn't do it.'

But still no one spoke.

'All right,' said Kate. 'Why don't you call the police? Or would you like me to do it for you?' She sprang to her feet and moved towards the telephone.

Cecil half-rose. 'Be careful, Kate. Holles is right. You should listen to his advice. You don't realise what you're saying.'

At that all the hope and expectation died out of her face.

'You, too?' she whispered, as though this was more than she could accept. '*You* believe him? But can't you understand—*everything* I've done has been for you. I haven't had a thought that wasn't rooted in you for twenty years. For you I've taken risks you can't conceive.'

'I only asked you to take one risk,' returned Cecil, steadily. 'That was twenty years ago, and you wouldn't take it. Ever since then it's been too late. There was nothing you could do for me. And now I've got Violet, who accepted a greater risk.'

What followed was as dreadful as murder itself. Indeed, to the more humane among them, to Cecil and to Isobel, it was like watching sudden death. The light in Kate's eyes went out as completely as the eastern sun sinks below the horizon, so that only darkness seemed to remain, the blood faded from her cheeks, old age seemed to fall upon her like a cloak, folding away from light for ever.

And out of that darkness her voice rose with the shock of some discordant wild bird.

'Violet? Violet take a greater risk than I? That shows how little you know. Would she have done what I did? I risked my very life to save your inheritance, the inheritance you say now has no value for you.'

Holles and Roger both turned towards her. But their words of counsel and their efforts to silence her were unavailing.

'You shall listen,' she cried. 'It doesn't matter any more what happens to me. The worst has happened already, but you shan't escape scot-free. Because the responsibility is yours as well as mine. Yes, I did it. She was going to speak, going to tell you all the truth—about the will. She *knew*, you see. Knew I'd burnt it. Ruth, she said. Oh, she'd been wicked, wicked for years, but that last wickedness, I thought, I could prevent. Weren't twenty years of both our lives enough for her? But no, she meant to steal the last thing of value I could save for you. Yes, that *I* could save. Not Violet, who has become your whole world. She was helpless. There was one risk she'd never have taken, but *I* took it, and when I'm in the condemned cell you can remember *why* I did it. That's how much I love you, Cecil. Think of me sometimes when you're happy with your wife and children and I'm—nothing, just a bagful of bones in the everlasting dark.'

'More likely in the nuthouse,' reflected Crook, but, before he could voice that or any other thought, Kate made a violent swerve, snatched at the handle of the door and was gone.

'Look out,' cried Crook, but he was too late. She was through the door, had slammed it and they all heard the key turn in the lock and the sound of her feet racing madly up the stairs.

Crook wasted no time struggling with the door. 'The windows!' he exclaimed, crossing the room and wrenching the curtains apart. 'How do these damned things open?'

'I'll show you.'

Nurse Alexander came to his side. Between them they got the window open and Crook clambered on to the sill.

'Not too much of a drop. One of you chaps ring the station.' He let himself go and vanished into the dark.

'Wait a minute,' called Nurse. 'I'm coming.'

'Regular circus,' grumbled Crook, steadying her as she came crashing down beside him. 'Come on, try the back door.'

'She's as mad as a hatter,' panted Nurse Alexander. 'Will they . . .?'

'Come on,' said Crook. 'We ain't the police, praise the pigs.'

The back door was fastened, but when they rattled the garden door it opened, and they went panting up the back stairs, like a pair of plump pussy-cats.

'Shall we be in time?' wondered Nurse. 'I suppose she's got some stuff.'

They reached Kate's door but that was locked, too, and though they hammered on it, and shouted her name furiously, there was no reply.

'She can't have taken anything that would act that fast,' muttered Nurse. She dropped to her plump haunches, and peered through the keyhole.

'I can't see anything.'

'Of course you can't. The key's in the lock.'

'What's that?' Nurse nearly fell over with surprise. Only Crook's hand on her plump shoulder kept her upright. 'No, it's not. I can see right through.'

Crook pushed her unceremoniously out of the way and ducked in his turn.

'She's fooled us,' he said, disgustedly. 'She's got all her wits about her, after all, knew we'd come pounding up here, so— she locked the door *on the outside* to fool us, delaying action they call it, and she's—where?'

'Lady Dingle's room,' gasped Nurse. 'She had sleeping-stuff.'

But there was no one in the big cold room, no one in the bathroom, no one in the attics.

Crook drew a deep breath. 'Tell me,' he said, 'is that garden door always open?'

'That's a funny thing,' said Nurse. 'Now I come to think of it, seeing the house is practically shut up, you'd have expected that to be locked.'

Crook nodded. 'So, now we know the way she went. What lies beyond the garden?'

'There's a little wood. You go through a door in the wall.'

'And then?'

'What they call the ornamental water.'

'How deep?'

'Deep enough,' said Nurse soberly. 'Do you think . . .?'

'Well, how does it look to you? You stay here, ring the

doctor, no, ring the police, tell 'em to send an ambulance.'

'I'm coming with you,' insisted Nurse. 'We might be in time.'

'The optimists women are,' protested Crook. 'O.K., come on.'

Kate, however, was taking no chances. The blue gate in the wall was locked and the wall itself was too high to be scaled even by a man a good deal younger than Mr Crook.

After that, even Nurse Alexander admitted defeat. Together they made their way back to the house.

They met Frank Hardy on the path. 'Did you get her?'

Crook shook his head. 'Why should we do the police's job for them? Is there a way round by the road? Gosh! When I think we sat round like a lot of dummies and let her walk out under our eyes.'

'You're not going to faint, are you?' demanded Nurse suspiciously.

'What, me?' demanded Crook, glowering. 'Be your age. Better turn your attention to Frank here. He looks as green as a gooseberry.'

'It's so beastly,' muttered Frank.

'It's murder,' corrected Crook. 'Murder's always beastly. Chaps like you think of it as a nice cosy yarn round the fire, or a game of chess. It's all baloney. Murder's a dirty job for everyone concerned, not a parlour-game. It's beastly for the corpse and it's beastly for the criminal, when he's caught. It's beastly for the police and the prison warders and the hangman. to say nothing of the judge and jury. Come to that, it's beastly for me, believe or no. And, of course,' he added coolly, 'it's not a piece of cake for Mrs Appleyard.'

'At least her name's cleared,' observed Frank. 'Thank goodness Holles was there. His evidence at all events won't be suspect.'

Nurse Alexander had the last word. 'Say what you like, she's saved everyone a lot of trouble taking this way out. Don't they say a prosecution for murder costs the country five thousand pounds?'

Some time later she said, 'Now, Mr Crook, you're a lawyer, tell me this. Does Ruth get that ten thousand, after all?'

Epilogue

'I told you to leave it to me,' said Crook.

He was talking to his latest client, newly released from gaol.

'I can still hardly believe it—that it was Kate,' confessed Ruth. 'I knew, of course, she was in love with Cecil, but I never thought—after thirty years. Poor Kate!'

'That's women all over,' said Crook, rather disgusted. 'She'd have let you swing, sugar, don't make any mistake about that.'

'Yes. I suppose she hated me all along. Isn't it a fact that some people virtually commit suicide, and if so wouldn't you say Lady Dingle was one of them?'

'Why ask me?' enquired Crook. 'I'm only a lawyer, I have to do things by rule of thumb, and I don't know anything about people committing suicide by proxy. Just common or garden crime's good enough for me. And if you're goin' to find an excuse for everyone who picks up a chopper or pushes some undesirable out of a window chaps like me are going on the dole. No, Kate Waring was a murderer, and if you tell me she smothered the old lady because she loved not wisely but too well, all I can say is thank heaven I'm no romantic. One thing, she's made Cecil Dingle look a rare fool. You can't learn too young, sugar, that chaps don't fall in love with dames who make sacrifices for them—what is that but slinging a millstone round their necks? The best thing you can say about Miss Waring is that nothing became her life as the leaving of it—and let it rest there. How about you, sugar? Got any plans?'

'I haven't had much time,' said Ruth. 'I can't believe prospective employers are going to fall over themselves to secure my services.'

'No getting away from the fact that wherever you go things happen,' Crook acknowledged. 'Heard from young Hardy?'

Her face stiffened. 'Why should I? He believed I was responsible for my husband's death and had most likely killed Lady Dingle.'

'Could be,' Crook acknowledged. 'On the other hand, he dragged me in, he suppressed evidence, he put himself in Dutch with the authorities—lucky for him he's got Canada to go back to.'

Ruth started. 'Oh—yes, of course. Not that it matters. No one's going to suggest he was—criminally involved.'

'You can't have been listening,' said Crook, patiently. 'Everyone believes just that. Well, be your age, honey. Rich girl, widow, probably a murderess, and he's backing her up to the hilt. Ain't it natural chaps should ask why, and answer their own question? It ain't been all fish and chips for Frank Hardy. As for the late Appleyard,' he went on deliberately, 'say you read the story and it was someone else's, how would it seem to you?'

'I don't know,' said Ruth, wearily. 'I've thought so often about him lately. But I don't know any more than I did the day he died.'

As she spoke, she seemed to Crook to change back to the girl whose happiness had been destroyed all in a moment by a man's criminal carelessness. Once again she relived that endless vigil at the Italian villa. At first it had seemed obvious that he had got tired of waiting and gone off to keep his rendezvous with the other woman—Bianca was her name, Ruth had discovered after his death. She had thought of packing a bag and being gone before his return, but love doesn't die so easily, and four years of happiness can't be blotted out in five minutes. So she had sat, waiting and remembering, until she recalled the car in the road and went down to the gate and made her momentous discovery that it had gone. Even now she could only guess at where the truth lay. Had he, after all, been sunbathing in a remote corner of the garden, he who adored the sun, and slipped away, not wanting to be questioned, not wanting to miss any more of his tawdry little adventure, angry, perhaps, because she, Ruth, had come back later than she promised? Perhaps he had called out and she hadn't heard. She would never know. And when he died, what had his last thought been—of her? or Bianca? or the desperate knowledge that this was the end, that he couldn't save himself, he who loved life and made it blossom.

Suddenly Ruth put her head down on her hands and wept. For the first time she wept not for herself and love betrayed and faith mocked, but for Jack, who'd had to pay so heavily for a bill he'd run up on the spur of the minute, and probably hadn't mattered very much to him anyhow.

'I wouldn't have done that to Jack,' she said at last. 'I loved him, I'd have fought for him. I mightn't have won, but at least I'd have tried.'

'I believe you, honey,' said Crook. 'Same as Fogg never believed you tried to do for your old man.'

'I used to think sometimes that perhaps one day, on his death-bed, my father would admit the truth, that it was a trap. After all, no one could have hurt him then, and he'd hurt me so much. But he never said a word, or if he did no one ever told me.'

'No,' said Crook soberly. 'I don't suppose he ever said it. You'd got the better of him, you see, and you'd gone on and been happy. He'd find it pretty hard to forgive you for that. He looked so silly, you see. Sugar, do you think about it much now?'

'I didn't when I had Jack. He was like the sun. And now it's gone in.'

'It'll come out again,' Crook assured her. 'Of course it will. Who the heck are you to disturb the natural rhythm of the universe? There's times I wonder why I went in for the law,' he added, reflectively. 'I could make a packet shooting my mouth off on a soap-box. And now dry your eyes and put that stuff on your face women seem to think it's indecent to go without, because you've got a visitor coming, and even if you're only going to say good-bye, there's no harm looking your best.'

He went out and leaned over the banisters. 'Come up, Frank,' he said.

Frank Hardy walked into the room.

'Why have you come?' asked Ruth, when Crook had taken his departure.

'You didn't answer any of my letters.'

Ruth stared. 'You never wrote me any.'

'I did. A dozen at least.'

'I never had them, not even one.'

'Well,' confessed Frank, 'I never posted them—not even one. Oh Ruth, it's no good lying. I did think perhaps you were guilty, both in Italy and down at Dingle Hall, but, even if I still doubted you, it wouldn't have made any difference to the way I feel, because I love you for the person you are. I told you you'd got under my skin, from that first afternoon. I want you to marry me and come to Canada with me. It's a big place, the name of Ruth Appleyard won't mean a thing there to anyone.'

'Not even to you?' asked Ruth gently. 'Mr Crook's right. Wherever I am things happen. Aren't you afraid something might happen to you?'

'Oh, all marriage is chancy,' Frank agreed. 'For all you know, I'm the Bluebeard of Canada, but you've got to risk it. And don't imagine that by refusing to marry me you're going to escape danger. There's only one safe place and that's the grave. Wouldn't even marriage with me be better than that?'

In the kitchen of a pleasant flat in South Kensington, Nurse Alexander put four spoonsful of tea from the Coronation tea-caddy into a handsome silver pot and poured on the boiling water. While she waited for the mixture to draw she picked up a letter that had just arrived by the afternoon post. The signature was Ruth Hardy.

'That girl!' she said in admiring tones, beginning to pile cups on to a tray. 'She does get about. One minute she's a penniless companion, then she's a prospective heiress, then she's in gaol for murder and now she's off to Canada with a new husband. Never a dull moment. And Violet Dingle's going to have twins—that 'ud make the old lady turn in her grave—next thing we shall hear of Mr Crook getting married.' She caught sight of her own buxom face in a glass hanging on the wall. 'And I don't mind telling you, Ada, my girl,' she confided to it, 'you could do a lot worse.'

169

She jammed a woollen tea-cosy shaped like a hen over the pot.

'And so could he,' she told it, 'only he'd never think of anything so sensible. Men!'

She picked up the tray and carried it off as triumphantly as if it were something she'd netted in a jungle for the benefit of her new patient.

>>> If you've enjoyed this book and would like to discover more great vintage crime and thriller titles, as well as the most exciting crime and thriller authors writing today, visit: >>>

The Murder Room
Where Criminal Minds Meet

themurderroom.com

www.ingramcontent.com/pod-product-compliance
Ingram Content Group UK Ltd.
Pitfield, Milton Keynes, MK11 3LW, UK
UKHW022309280225
455674UK00004B/240